ISA'S INSULIN

Chester Gattle

For Martha and Pam
Your counsel was invaluable

I

The Boy

I was heading inside the Superette, a corner store near my house, when Carlos called me over.

"There's a guy I'm looking for," he said.

I stepped up to the rusting Chevrolet Caprice and gave him an uncertain look. "A guy?"

"Yeah." He rolled his window down the rest of the way. A cloud of cologne wafted out. "Supposed to be coming through here sometime in the next hour. I don't have time to hang around. Busy morning, you know? Can you watch for him? Be a big favor." He adjusted his sunglasses, a set of silver aviators. "Big favor."

My reflection loomed monstrously in the clean silver of his sunglasses. "Sure," I said as the stretched reflection gave a nod.

Carlos smiled wide, teeth somehow perfectly, naturally straight. "Awesome, dude. So he'll be driving a van, right?"

I nodded.

"Big and boxy. Green all over except for the front doors. Those are white. And the guy's old. Forty, maybe. With a goatee." He took a second to think, then added, "And he has those eyeglasses that don't have any frames. Not sure you can tell that from here, but whatever." Carlos handed me a thin walkie-talkie. "Just hang around until you see the guy, okay?"

I turned the electronic over in my hands, dragging a finger over the touchpad. "Why's it have so many buttons?"

"What're you talking about? That's how cell phones are."

"It's not a walkie-talkie?" I pushed a random button, causing the screen to light up with a greenish glow.

"No. It's a Nokia."

"How's it work?"

"Doesn't matter. Now listen. When you see the guy,"—Carlos reached out and touched the phone's keypad—"hit TALK. TALK," he repeated. "I've already got the number punched in. Just hit TALK. Okay?"

"And then what?"

"Done deal. I'll owe you."

"You'll owe me?"

"I'll owe you."

"Cool."

Carlos flashed his Hollywood smile. "Gotta go, dude. Catch you later." He reversed out of the spot and left me there holding the phone.

I walked back to my dirt bike, a Frankenstein project I'd saved from the dump. I'd leaned it against a utility pole that someone had painted pink and marked with a black cross in remembrance of "Paul." I sat sideways on the bike, making the springs creak, and tugged at my shirt for a breeze. No wonder Carlos hadn't wanted to sit around. The sun was a killer. The fruit cart guy on the corner was slicing and chopping under the shade of a couple of palm trees, but his face was streaked with sweat.

But at least I wasn't the man across the street leaning a ladder against the pharmacy building. As a mother and her daughter walked around him and vanished inside, he hiked up his work belt and started up to the baking rooftop.

I pushed the sand around with my feet, forming it into a smiley face, then wiped the drawing from existence. I did this about a dozen times until the van finally came rolling down the street. I couldn't tell if the man's eyeglasses were frameless (just like Carlos had suspected), but everything else matched, and in the morning heat, that was good enough for me.

I pushed the TALK button just as the van stopped at the intersection. There were a couple rings, then someone picked up.

"We good?" some man asked.

"I think so," I answered, squinting, double-checking the van. "Yeah, I think so."

The line went dead.

"Hello?" I checked the screen. It just showed the time in blocky text. "Crap." I'd lost the connection. I'd have to follow the van. No way was I going to screw this up for Carlos. He'd never ask me to do anything again.

But right before I jumped on my little dirt bike, two souped-up bikes came blasting around the corner, racing down the street.

They skidded to a stop beside the van, and the riders raised their rifles.

Pop-pop-pop!

The fruit vendor dove for cover. People scrambled into the Superette. A stray dog sprinted by me, a line of pee trailing it.

The gunfire stopped as the stoplight changed from red to green. The van stayed where it was. The driver, his head tilted to the sky, didn't move.

The riders leaned forward on their bikes and tore off down an alley.

"Jesus." I stood there, phone in my hand, holding my breath.

Eventually, a few people came out of the store. The fruit vendor picked himself up off the ground. The mother-daughter duo poked their heads from the pharmacy as the service man peered over the rooftop, pliers in hand.

I grabbed my bike and walked it away. No way in hell was I starting it up then.

Not that anyone was going to come chasing after me or pointing an accusing finger my way. People didn't do that. Everyone kept their mouths shut. By the time the police arrived, there'd be a crowd gathered around the van as courage and curiosity grew, but there'd be no talking, ever.

Carlos and I probably wouldn't even say anything to each other. He'd just give me some cash, and we'd call it even.

I went off down the street hoping it'd be a decent amount. I'd just gotten a guy killed, after all.

II

The Trafficker

While the croissant rotated around in the microwave, the slab of honey butter atop it turned soft and shiny, and then slid off.

I couldn't help think of the migrants heating up in the back of that semi-trailer.

They'd all be dead within a day.

The driver I'd hired to take those poor suckers north had gotten spooked by a string of state troopers watching for speeders. He'd ditched the trailer somewhere along I-20 between Odessa and Dallas.

I should've known better. The guy had been too green. That haul wasn't for rookies.

But nothing I could do about it now. No time. Without ventilation, those migrants weren't going to last any longer than honey butter.

I pulled the croissant from the microwave, being careful not to burn my thumb on the sticky corner hanging over the side of the plate, and walked over to the window. El Paso stretched out before me from my perch up on the west side of the Franklin Mountains.

Ruler of everything I could see.

Or so that was the dream. I could see plenty of Juárez, but I wasn't allowed to touch that. Not right now.

I picked up the dripping croissant and bit off half of it, calculating how many more reps on the bench press I'd need to do to get rid of these stress carbs.

Idiot drivers leading to dead migrants leading to stress carbs.

News of the trailer would be in the paper tomorrow as the media tripped over itself to report on the migrants' misfortunes. The headlines would be sensationalistic and horrifying. Fodder for their readership, the disaster whores that they were.

"Fuckers," I grumbled, chewing.

If the public didn't have this sick fascination with death and disaster, I could just go back to work, but once the news picked up the story, people would holler and yell. There'd be an investigation (which didn't matter all that much since the trailer's tags were forged and there was nothing else to lead the police to the "bad guys"), but then they'd tighten border security, and that pissed me off. The border agents would get pressured to increase their inspection rates, and the slow-ass speed at which traffic moved across the border would come to a standstill. My throughput would drop by half. Yes, I could use the tunnels, but I hated those things. They were so poorly constructed. I lost more than I got through.

So this idiot driver, this Moses Rose, was going to cost me a million dollars, easily, because the next few months were now utterly and completely shot.

To top it off, that wasn't even why I was eating the stress carbs that morning. Word was that my partner in Juárez wanted me dead.

III

The Sicario

"Tip your head to the side." My brother was standing in front of the Rio Grande's concrete-lined channel, and there was this cool charcoal-colored stain down the side of it that I wanted to get in the picture. "And don't smile."

"Why can't I smile?" Nemesio asked.

"You look like a dork."

His face turned to stone; I clicked the button.

"Here." I gave him the disposable camera, and we switched places.

After he'd taken a few shots of me, he came over to the rail, and we looked at the greasy stain where the body had landed, where there was a sooty splatter, like a water balloon filled with black ink had burst.

"When you think they took it away?" Nemesio asked, handing me back the camera.

I checked the dial on the Kodak to make sure we had enough pictures left. "Probably right away. Why would they just leave a burning body?"

"They leave people hanging from the bridges."

"Not for long."

We stared for a little longer. The wind picked up.

"I can smell it."

"No, you can't."

"Smells like ass."

"Whatever."

"It does."

I went back to our dad's Mercedes S-Class. "Let's go," I shouted.

He glanced at the channel once more, then hurried over. "How we doing on time?" he asked as I sped off toward the nail salon.

"Fine if Dad hadn't been such a dick about the car," I said, veering through traffic.

"How much more you need for the Armada?"

"Not much." I zipped through a bunch of lights. A yellow one, a red one, another yellow, then turned into the Pemex station across from the ugly magenta-colored salon and backed into a spot far from the pumps.

Nemesio pointed at a polished, pearl-white truck on the corner. "That's her, isn't it?"

"It's her *truck*. Not her," I corrected.

"That's what I said."

"No you didn't." I leaned over the steering wheel. "Why's a bitch like her even getting her nails done?"

"BB tells her to."

"BB's such a scuzz."

He laughed. "Yeah. A scuzz."

BB was this low-life dealer trying to turn trafficker who we'd introduced to our friend, one of the best coyotes in El Paso, a few months ago, but things weren't working out between them.

Nemesio reached under his seat and pulled out a 9mm Pietro Beretta, then grabbed a roll of duct tape he'd stashed in the glove compartment. He held it close to his nose. "I love the smell of new tape."

I did too, but I didn't say anything. I was getting mesmerized by one of those large plastic sidewalk signs outside the salon as it wobbled back and forth in the dry wind. After a few minutes, I blinked hard and leaned back. "How long do nails take?"

My brother shrugged and started fiddling with the edge of the duct tape, peeling it, breathing deep, pressing it back, peeling it, breathing, pressing it back.

I cranked the air conditioning, and we waited for what felt like forever. Finally, the bitch stepped out of the salon, looking all smug, pulling her sunglasses down over her eyes like she was some princess.

I hit my brother across the shoulder. "Here we go."

The woman—skimpy tank top and distressed designer jeans—started toward her truck, and I rocketed the car from the parking spot and across the boulevard. I tried to pull off a cool sideways slide into the curb, but I hit the brakes too late, and we bounced up and over it, halfway onto the sidewalk.

Nemesio's gun flew from his hand and clattered around the dash. He quickly grabbed it, then jumped out.

BB's bitch yanked out a canister of pepper spray from her purse, screaming, "Get back. Get away."

Nemesio halted midstep, his gun at his side. "Don't you fucking dare," he warned.

"Don't *you* fucking dare," the woman said.

I smirked. Nemesio was so short that the woman was actually pointing the pepper spray *down* into my brother's face. But then I realized I was shorter than my *younger* brother, and the smirk fell away.

"Just come on. Come with us," Nemesio said. "We won't hurt you."

"Leave me alone, or you're dead," she hissed.

"Come on, lady. This isn't even about you. It's

about BB."

She shook the pepper spray. "Get away."

"Come on."

"Get away, asshole."

Nemesio turned back to me. "She's not coming."

"Yeah. I can see that."

"What do I do?"

I stepped out of the car and looked over the roof at the woman. "Just get in the car, okay?"

She shook her head. She looked around, then spotted a truck coming down the street. She raised her hands and started waving them. "Help," she called out. "Hey!" She was bouncing in her heels, not really jumping, just bouncing.

I gestured at Nemesio. "Go ahead."

He grunted, turned to the woman, and emptied his gun into her, sending her stumbling back, falling over the sidewalk sign. The canister went rolling from her hand.

I came around the car. "Why don't they just come?" I took a few photos with the disposable camera, then reached down and twisted the woman's turquoise ring from her pinky.

"Probably 'cause they know we're lying," Nemesio said.

"About what?"

"Hurting 'em."

I pocketed the ring and stared down the street at the truck that'd been coming our way. It was just sitting there. I couldn't see the driver with the windshield glare, but I was sure we were looking at each other. I shook my head, and the truck made a U-turn and sped away.

"If they know who we are," Nemesio said, "they *have* to know what's coming."

I laughed. "Hermanos de la Muerte."

IV

The Boy

My house sat on the edge of a ridge on a street called Joaquín Terrazas, overlooking the dry expanse that was Juárez. Evening shadows were creeping around flat-roofed, single-story buildings for as far as I could see.

To the left, to the north, there was El Paso, but from up on Joaquín Terrazas, the cities looked like the single sprawling metropolis they had once been.

Paso del Norte, a desert passage between the mountains.

And the Rio Grande was just a river in the middle of it all.

I rested my bike against the side of the house and stared up at a bird on the tangled mess of electrical wires the neighbors had strung up. The utility company wanted to charge for electricity, but the neighbors had their workaround. I wanted to hang a line too, but my mom and grandma wouldn't let me. They apparently liked getting the electricity cut off when we couldn't pay the bill.

The bird jumped from wire to wire, finally settling on the single black one that ran to my pale stucco house, mocking me.

I waved my hands at it until the bird flew off.

Across the street, Carlos's house had lines shooting off in every direction. He wasn't paying for anything. He knew what was up. I thought about going over and giving him back his phone, but his gunmetal Caprice was nowhere in sight, so I went inside. Dinner had to be about ready. I could smell the pozole.

Isa, my youngest sister, was on the couch, her feet barely reaching the edge of the cushion. She smiled, creasing the red-wine birthmark on her cheek.

"Get your homework done?" I went over and nudged one of the frayed textbooks she had on the floor.

"Almost," she sighed.

"Need any help?"

A flip of her ponytail. "No, thanks." She returned to the multiplication table resting on the deflated cushion.

I'd gotten straight As when I had gone to school.

Kind of a pointless success.

Like me, Isa wasn't going to continue on past the sixth grade. She *thought* she was going to grow up to be a teacher or a doctor or whatever else seemed fun, but I knew better. I saw how it all worked.

We needed money, not report cards.

And now that I was old enough to get some work, I did, usually washing cars at the roundabout or selling paletas near the border. Or if that wasn't available, like today, I wandered around, looking for discarded items that might still have some value.

"I'll help if you need it," I said, turning away. "Just let me know."

"Okay."

The kitchen doorway was decorated with drawings

Isa and my other sister, Katie, had tacked up. There was a new one among the rainbows, flowers, and smiling bears of a little girl with a bow in her hair. Floating beside the girl was a giant, pink needle.

"Is this you?" I asked Isa.

"Uh-huh."

"How're you doing on your insulin?"

"Hmm. I have a couple days left."

"We'll get you some more before you run out."

She didn't look like she believed me. And I wasn't certain of what I said either. It depended on what work I could get tomorrow and the next. And also if Carlos paid me for what I'd helped him with earlier. He was usually generous, but I couldn't count on anything until the money was in my hands.

"We'll get more," I repeated, then disappeared into the kitchen before I said, "promise."

My grandma and Katie were at the counter near the sink, cutting onions.

"You go where I told you to go?" my grandma asked without looking up.

"Yes, ma'am." She was talking about the mineshaft up in the mountains. She'd heard from her old lady friends that it could be a good place to search. They thought there might be hordes of forgotten tools I could clean up and sell, but it had been a huge waste of time.

"And?" she pressed.

"I found a hammer."

She clucked her tongue. "That's it?"

"That's it."

"Shame."

"I tried. I was there for hours."

She didn't hear. The radio—a little thing I'd found in the dump last month—was on the shelf next to her and had started belting out some love ballad. She went on cutting, and I ducked into the windowless closet that we called a bathroom.

When I stepped out, the song was fading, and she asked, "How about my flour?"

I stared out the kitchen window. The view was hazy and drab during the day, but now that the sun was setting and the wind dying down so the dust could settle, the city lights were starting to sparkle.

"Well?" she pressed.

I said, "I forgot," but that's why I'd been at the Superette in the first place.

"A memory as bad as your grandfather's," she grumbled. "You're lucky I don't need it tonight. Go tomorrow morning."

"Yes, ma'am."

Neither she nor Katie seemed to notice that a narcocorrido, *Producto Garantizado*, was now playing on the radio, so I pretended not to notice too, but when my mom got home a minute later, the first thing she did was turn the radio off.

"You shouldn't let the kids listen to those songs," she said as she sat down at the table.

"I wasn't even paying attention to it," my grandma said, scooping a big pile of onions into the stew.

"Well, they pay attention to it." My mom took off the hat the maquiladora made her wear, and her hair fell in strings across her face.

I grabbed a hair tie from a drawer and handed it to her. "You get to eat lunch today?"

It was a stupid question. I shouldn't have asked it. Nobody took breaks at the maquiladoras. I was just hoping she wouldn't shake her head.

I helped Katie set the table, and a couple of minutes later, we had our dinner together in the small house that overlooked the city.

V

The Boy

The next day I grabbed a spot washing cars at the roundabout near the Anapra barrio, and did that for about ten hours, walking away with a couple dollars for the work.

Closer to Isa's insulin.

We'd get there.

I hopped on my bike and raced through the city streets, turning the desert air into a nice breeze. By the time I slowed and turned onto Joaquín Terrazas, there wasn't a drop of soapy sweat left on me.

Carlos was outside his house near his rusty Caprice, fiddling with his keys. He looked up and gestured for me to come over.

"Good job yesterday," he said, flashing his perfect teeth.

I rubbed at a smudge on the bike's handlebars. "Yeah. No biggie."

"You got my phone?"

I pulled the Nokia from a compartment under the seat.

He took it and pressed a few buttons with fingers covered in small black tattoos. Stars and feathers and skulls. He glanced up, smiled. "Talk to anyone about it?"

"No. No way." I sat back on the bike and shook my head. "No."

"Good." He tossed me the phone. "Keep it."

"Keep it?"

"Might as well. And here." He pulled ten dollars from his wallet.

"Sweet."

"Yeah. Good job. So you up for some more?"

"Of what?"

He walked around me to the back of his car. "You not up for it?"

"No, no. I'm up for it."

"Cool." He popped the trunk and yanked out a dark backpack. "Just take this to the park on Berilio. You know, the one with that shitty mural of tomato juice or something?"

"Over there?" I pointed beyond my house.

"Yep. Couple blocks that way." He threw me the pack, which looked and felt empty. "You're meeting a guy named JP. JP's got a backpack for you. Give him yours. Take his."

"That's it?"

"Simple." He slammed the trunk and came back around, jingling his keys in his hand.

"What's JP look like?"

Carlos gave it some thought but eventually just said, "A junkie, I guess."

"There's a lot of junkies." I pointed at a scarecrow of a guy down the block as proof.

"It's the park on Berilio. You two will probably be the only ones there."

I shrugged. That was true. Nobody went to that park anymore.

"Don't worry," Carlos said. "Just go over there in about ten minutes and chill, okay?"

I looked at him, then his car, then back at him.

"I'll owe you. Big."

I grinned. "Yeah. Okay."

"Great." He flung open his car door. "Gotta go. Gotta jet."

I watched him leave, then walked my bike across Joaquín Terrazas and up to my house. As I headed inside, I was thinking if no one was home, I'd take a look into the pack. I knew what was in it, but I just wanted to see. Juárez was a one of several gateway cities for the billions of dollars of drugs that flowed over the border every year, and I wanted to see some of it close up.

The moment I stepped through the front door, though, I realized that wasn't happening.

My sister was sitting cross-legged in the middle of the kitchen floor with a jar of peaches in her lap. "Can you open this?" she asked. "I'm low."

"How low?" I hurried over and took the jar.

"I don't know. I'm out."

She meant she was out of her glucose test strips, so she had no way to know precisely how low her blood sugar was other than just feeling it. Shaky. Sweaty. Nauseous. I popped the jar open. "Do you want me to get a couple out for you?"

"No." She plunged a hand into the fruit and syrup, fishing around until she'd captured a slice, then popped the whole thing into her mouth. Then another. She grabbed a third but held it in her fist, chewing and chewing with cheeks bulging.

The hand holding the peach was shaking. Tiny tremors. Drops of syrup fell from the bottom of her fist and onto her sundress. Lows weren't usually a big deal, she just needed to eat some sugar, some carbs, but they could get bad if she didn't quickly take care of them. (She had passed out once, and Grandma had to give her a shot of glucagon.)

"Are you okay?" I asked, setting the jar beside her.

"Yeah." She went on chewing.

"Where's Grandma?"

"Napping."

"Katie too?"

She nodded slightly. "Yeah."

"We'll get you more supplies soon. Insulin and strips."

She looked down at the jar of peaches.

I sat next to her and ate one of the fruit slices myself. After several minutes, her hands steadied. "I have to go," I said, squeezing her little shoulder. "Just have to run somewhere quick."

She dug in for another peach. "Where?"

"Just...somewhere. Be back in a bit." I grabbed Carlos's pack from the floor.

The park, a dried-out block of brown earth and leafless trees, was empty when I got there. I pulled up next to the building with the juice mural that Carlos thought was shitty. (I didn't disagree. The lower half of the mural was spray painted with so many gang symbols and messages that it looked like a little kid had scribbled all over it. The glass of juice sat buried in a spaghetti- mess of black swirls.)

Across the street, cracked pathways that nobody walked on anymore and plastic benches that nobody sat on anymore bisected the square. Off in a corner was a swing set that sat motionless.

Bad things had happened in this park.

A couple girls had been abducted. A boy my age had been shot. Some addict had buried her three-year-old in the sand under the swings. Alive.

The sedan in front of me hadn't been moved in a while. Its back window had been smashed out and its tires were flat.

It wasn't hard to spot the man I was supposed to meet when he came pedaling up on his bicycle. He stopped on the far side of the park, laid the bike in the dirt, and made his way down the pathway, head low, swinging bony arms splashed with tattoos.

I went to meet him in the center of the park. "JP?" I asked.

The man kept his head down, the brim of his baseball hat covering his eyes.

"Carlos said to meet you."

The tattoos climbing up the guy's arms disappeared under his shirt, becoming vague shapes beneath the thin fabric, stretching all the way across his chest and stomach.

"You JP?"

The man lifted his head slightly, and his eyes momentarily settled on me and the pack over my shoulder. "Hand it over," he said just before his eyes lost their focus and began to swim around, taking in the world but not really. The guy gestured with a shaky, outstretched hand. "Give it."

"You're JP?" I slipped the pack from my shoulder.

The man grabbed for it, missed, then tried again, his fingers skittering across the black canvas before clamping down.

I let him have it.

He pulled the pack to his chest, then turned and started back the way he'd come.

"Hey. Hang on," I yelled.

The man stopped. He glanced over his shoulder.

"You're supposed to give me the other one." I pointed at the pack he'd brought.

The man sneered. "Supposed to?"

"Yeah." I stepped closer. "That's the deal, isn't it?"

He slipped the pack off his shoulder and let it fall to the ground. "Is it?"

"Yeah." I reached down for the pack, but the man spun around with a squeal and slashed the air with a knife, missing me by an inch.

The man's eyes went wide with fury, and he lunged forward, jabbing the knife in my direction, but I wasn't there anymore. I had already sidestepped him, and I punched him hard on the side of his head, sending his cap flying.

He wobbled, shuffled his feet but regained his balance and swiped at me again. So I swung again, cracking him across the jaw. I threw another punch, but the man was already going down, crumpling at my feet, and my fist passed over his head with a whoosh.

The guy was still holding the knife, though, so I dropped onto his back and dug my knees into his neck. "Let go."

"No." The man tried swiping at me with the knife, but his arm wouldn't bend at the odd angle he needed it to.

I jammed my knees harder into his neck.

"No," he cried, but he had already opened his hand and let the knife fall away.

I grabbed it from the dirt and stood. "Why'd you do that?"

The man rolled over, wheezing, chuckling. "Bitches get stitches." He laughed loud at the sky, eyes cloudy and unfocused. "Just trying to get some meth, man. Little for me. Little to sell. You know? God's truth." He pointed a finger up at the sky.

I put my foot near his face and watched his eyes turn to it. "Get up." I nudged his shoulder. "Just get out of here."

He grunted and rolled himself over. He reached for the backpacks, but I shoved him away.

"What about our deal?" he complained, picking himself up.

"Tough shit." I pointed the knife at him.

He gritted his teeth, but he couldn't do anything and he knew it. He turned and hurried back to his bicycle. "You're an asshole," he shouted as he pedaled off.

VI

The Boy

The next day, after my mom had gotten on the bus to the maquiladora where she stitched together car upholstery, and my grandma had left to walk Isa and Katie to school (because little girls should never walk by themselves in Juárez), I sat on the couch, staring at my dad's uniform hanging on the wall. There was a medal pinned to the breast, a gold star with a white-and-red ribbon, and I had been told it was in recognition of his valor. It'd been awarded posthumously.

He had always been chasing the cartels, catching traffickers, seizing drug shipments. He was one of the best. Every year he found more. More drugs. More guns. More cash. I waited for the day when he'd come home and say, "I got it all. It's over now."

But it was an endless conveyor belt of drugs, and he was just grabbing bits and pieces as it sped past. Sometimes the conveyer belt would slow—the US would tighten the border for a day or a week or a month—and he'd get more of it, thousands of kilos of it, but even then, he wasn't really getting anything.

"There are buildings," he'd say, "cavernous buildings along the border, and each one is filled with drugs. But tomorrow..." He'd hold up a fist, leave it for a moment, then snap open his fingers. "Poof. It'll be all gone."

I got up from the couch and walked to the uniform, leaning close, examining the medal, thinking it could be worth a vial of insulin or two if it was real gold, wondering if we'd sell it someday if things got bad enough.

I had put the ten dollars from Carlos in an envelope that we kept tucked under the mattress in the bedroom. I hadn't counted what was in the envelope, though. It was always too little.

Just had to keep putting money in there.

I flopped back onto the couch, taking a look at the phone Carlos had given me. It probably had some value, but before I could think in any seriousness about how much I could get for it, the phone started ringing with a chirpy Mozart chime.

"Hello?"

"Knock, knock," Carlos said.

"What do you mean?"

There was a knock on the front door

I spun around. "Is that you?"

"'Course it is," he said. "Open up."

"Is it really?"

"What do you think?" he yelled from outside of the house.

I opened the door. "Just have to be sure. Break-ins and stuff, you know?"

"Yeah, yeah." He was grinning big. "Evaristo sends his compliments."

"Who's that?"

"The guy I had watching you yesterday." He leaned

to the side to see around me. "Anybody home?"

"Not right now."

"Cool." He kept leaning, searching the house. "Where're the packs?"

"Just over here." I went to the couch and lifted the cushions, pulling the backpacks from their hiding spot. "I know you said to trade with the guy, but—"

"But JP got feisty. I know." Carlos came in and took the backpacks. He inspected one, then the other, carefully checking their contents. "Don't worry about it. This was a big help." He tilted JP's pack to show me the wads of cash inside. "JP's with that crew over in Postal. We owed them for something a few weeks ago. There was this guy with this thing... But anyway, JP's not supposed to be making these kinds of trades, and his crew just needed a little confirmation of what he was doing." Carlos gave me a slap on the shoulder. "Good job."

"So you don't care if I took both?"

"No problem-o. JP's a bitch. Anybody pulls a knife on you, you kick their ass. Every time."

Shrugging, I said, "I guess."

He looked me up and down. "No 'I guess.' You do. *Especially* you. Use that muscle."

"I don't want to get in trouble, though."

"Pfft. You're a grown-ass man. What do you care?"

"I'm just thirteen."

"Shit. I thought you were my age."

I shook my head. "Thirteen."

"You're huge. How's that possible?"

"Lucky?"

"I have to put you to work. Take advantage of this."

"I don't want to get in trouble," I repeated.

"Nah, dude. You're not getting in trouble. Not for anything. Law says anyone under fourteen is 'not aware of their actions.' You could literally murder someone, and nothing would happen."

"I'm almost fourteen."

"But you're not. When you turn fourteen?"

"A couple weeks."

"Yeah, we need to get to work." Carlos grabbed a handful of bills from the backpack, then looked at me. "You swipe any of this?"

"Didn't even look inside 'em."

"Smart." Carlos shoved ten five-dollar bills into my hand. "Here."

"Really?" I clutched the money tight as if Carlos might change his mind and take back what was surely more than enough for Isa's insulin. There'd even be some left over, which was perfect, because Katie also had a birthday coming up, and I could surprise her with something.

"You earned it." Carlos backhanded me lightly on the chest. "Now let's go hit the street." He headed for the door.

"What're we doing?" I shoved the cash into my pocket and followed him out.

"You're going to be my muscle," he said as I locked the door.

"Wait," I called out. "Muscle?" I caught up to him as he was heading across the street to his Caprice. "I kind of don't want to fight again. Even if I won't get in trouble."

He laughed as he climbed into his car. "But you're undefeated."

"What if we get hurt?"

He looked up at me. "Hey, if you don't want to help, fine. It's basically free money, though." He shut the door and started the car.

"Wait. I was just asking." I hurried around and got in. "I can help."

"My dude," Carlos said and shifted into drive.

After a few blocks, Carlos pointed at a kid sitting on a lime-colored bicycle down at the next intersection.

"You need me for him?" I asked.

"The kid's a maniac." Carlos leaned forward, eyeing the boy. "Actually, I don't think he's talking today. Look at him. He's going to bolt."

He did look a bit like a rabbit in the desert, ears perked up, eyes frozen wide.

Carlos rolled up, and just as he had predicted, the kid planted his feet on the pedals and took off, disappearing behind some houses.

"Little fucker," Carlos muttered. "His loss. You don't get paid if you don't talk to me. Not paying a halcon who doesn't talk."

"Talk about what?" I asked.

"Just stuff. Whatever's out there."

A couple of blocks later, we found a chunky man wobbling along the edge of the road with a fruit cart. A line of footprints and tire tracks trailed behind him in the dust and trash that was piled up against the curb.

Carlos pulled over. "Roll your window down," he told me.

The fruit cart man leaned in and rested an arm on my door, breathing heavily through his mouth. "Hot today, Carlos," he said.

"Naranja, how's business?" Carlos asked.

"Fruit is fresh. People can't say no to fruit when it's fresh." Naranja gave one of his bushy sideburns a healthy scratch while he looked me over, then turned back at Carlos. "You want something?"

"Any kiwis?" Carlos asked.

"No. Still can't get them. I'm trying, though. I know you like them."

"Hold some for me when you get them."

"Yeah, yeah, of course."

"So what's new?"

The man lowered his voice. "Aztecas are collecting."

"For?"

"Not sure, but they're collecting."

"Guns," Carlos said to me. Then to Naranja: "So no word on what they're planning?"

"Zip. I'll let you know when I hear something, though. First thing."

"Good." Carlos leaned across the car, handing Naranja some cash.

The man thanked him, then grabbed two apples from his cart. "Got these this morning. They're good. Crispy."

Carlos took the fruit—"Thanks, man"—and moved on.

When we found the next halcon, Carlos said, "This one's sketchy. This one's why you're here."

I sat up and got myself ready, but when we pulled over, the man actually took a couple of steps back. He rested on a half-collapsed stone wall that wasn't doing a good job of protecting the squat house on the other side of it. The man scratched his arms, scabbed and red, waiting while I rolled down the window once again.

"Willy," Carlos called out. "How you doing?"

The man grinned deliriously wide, exposing crooked teeth and a darkened rot between them.

"Good, huh?" Carlos said. "You seeing anything?"

The man looked left, then right before shrugging and smiling again.

Carlos pulled a ball of plastic from his pocket and shoved it into my hand. "Toss it out to him."

I gave it a fling, and the man scrambled for it like a squirrel after a nut.

Carlos asked again, "You seeing anything?"

The man's eyes narrowed. "Aztecas."

"They bothering you?"

"Sometimes."

"Don't let them get you."

The man gave a furious nod.

"Anything else?"

"Hmm, no." The man suddenly jumped off the wall, causing Carlos to stiffen and me to do the same, but then Willy was gone, running past the front of the car and across the street, vanishing over another wall and around a corner.

Carlos said, "You wouldn't believe the strength those guys can muster. And they can take a beating. It's like they're made out of beef jerky or something. Just chew and chew and chew." Carlos turned to me. "You eat this morning?"

"No. You want the apples?" I reached into the back of the car where Carlos had tossed them.

"I want a real breakfast." He put the car into drive and took off.

Less than a minute later, we were at a food stall on a block lined with food stalls. Carlos hadn't even stepped to the counter of La Que Sabrosa Quesadilla when the man working there reached out with two plates of food. No money was exchanged; only a nod given.

Carlos and I went to a table around the side of the building. He pushed a plate across to me.

"Was this free?" I asked.

"Nothing's ever free," Carlos said, biting into his quesadilla.

"You didn't pay him, though."

"Cash isn't the only way to buy things."

"I wish."

"I'm serious." Carlos held up his middle finger, showing me a tattoo of two As just below the nail. "We give him protection. He gives us food."

"AA is Artistas Asesinos?"

"Yep."

"What're you protecting him from?"

"Aztecas. La Línea. The Juárez Cartel. Anyone who tries to mess with him and the barrio. We have to watch out for it, you know?" Carlos leaned to the side, reached into his pocket, and pulled out a hundred-dollar bill. "Here. It's for today." He slid it across the table.

I quickly put my hand over the money. "You're joking."

"Nope." He got up, went around the front of the food stall, and came back with two bottles of Coke. I still had my hand on the bill. "Take it," he said. "Just don't blow it on drugs."

"It's for Isa," I said, squeezing the bill, pulling it close.

"That's generous of you."

"For her insulin." I tucked the money into my pocket, then bit off a chunk of the quesadilla.

"How much that cost?"

Chewing, I glanced up at the dusty sky. "It changes. It's a lot, though."

"Probably dirt cheap to make. Like meth or cocaine."

"Don't know. All the diabetes stuff is expensive. Test strips, insulin, needles."

"Needles? You inject it?"

"Every meal. Every day."

"Are her arms all messed up like Willy's?"

I shook my head, bit at the quesadilla. "The needles are small. You can't even see the hole. But the kids at her school still make fun of her. Call her an addict. Call her Insulin Isa."

Carlos snorted. "Kids suck. I remember kids called me Crazy Carlos."

"What for?"

"Because of this." He turned his wrist over to show me a bunch of pockmarks that trailed all the way up to the crook of his elbow.

"You did drugs?"

"Fuck no. These are bee stings."

I leaned close, inspecting the discolored, dimpled skin. "Bees?"

"Big bees. Hornets."

"There's so many."

"I know." He pulled his arm away and pointed at one particularly deep indentation. "That was the first one. Was an accident. The rest I did to myself. They're not as deep. See? I knew the sting was coming, so I was ready."

"You stung yourself?"

"For attention." He grabbed his Coke bottle, put it to his lips, and threw back his head.

"Why?"

Swallowing, he said, "Like I said, the first time was an accident. I'd been outside playing, found a hole in the ground, and messed with it." He shrugged. "I didn't know any better. When the hornet got me, I started screaming like I'd been shot. My mom came running out of the house, and for the first time in like forever, she actually took care of me. Gave me a washcloth. Put a streak of toothpaste on the sting. Bandaged it over. I loved it. All that attention. She never gave two shits about me. So, after that, when I wanted my mom to give me some attention, I'd go get stung. I'd put my arm over the hole"—he laid his forearm against the table—"and wait for one of the bees to get angry."

"How come your parents wouldn't pay attention to you?"

"They were addicts. Spaced out of their mind all the time." Carlos waved a dismissive hand at his scars. "But fuck that. Insulin, huh?" He popped the last bit of quesadilla into his mouth and washed it down with the Coke. "I can help with that. You keep helping me, I'll keep helping you. Get Isa all the insulin she needs."

"That'd be awesome."

"I know it would." Carlos stood up. "So how about we finish our drive?"

I nodded, shoveling the rest of my quesadilla into my mouth and grabbing my Coke.

VII

The Sicario

I had the photos developed by a buddy of mine, then gave
the one of BB's girl to a courier who took it up to Jonathan
in El Paso. When Jonathan called, there was a long pause
after I'd said, "Hello."

"Alvaro," he finally groaned. "I wanted you to
kidnap her."

"So that *was* her. Awesome."

"What's that supposed to mean?"

"Eh. You never know." I took a swig of my Sidral
Mundet. "Sometimes you shoot the wrong chick."

On the other side of the table, my brother mumbled,
"I've never shot the wrong one," as he picked at his
sandwich.

"You almost did. That girl last summer," I
reminded him.

"Oh, yeah." Nemesio took a bite of his sandwich, a
small pile of vegetables on his plate.

"Please don't tell me that," Jonathan said. "Please don't say that."

"What?" I asked. "It's not a big deal."

Nemesio emphatically nodded at this.

"If you're not going to take this seriously," Jonathan said, "then—"

"You sound like my dad."

"—I have other people I can use."

I rolled my eyes. "Relax. It's done. Soledad Herrera is gone." I tipped my head back and chugged the last of the soda, burped loud enough to get a chuckle from Nemesio, then said, "I took her pinky ring. You want to send it to BB? Give it to him at her funeral? That'd be funny."

My brother smiled big. "Savage."

"Just find BB," Jonathan said, "and get my money."

I tossed the empty bottle into the waste bin beside the kitchen counter. "Fine. Then we get our ten percent?" I was thinking of my Armada: light blue, tinted windows, and chrome hubcaps that would keep spinning even when the car was stopped.

"If you jokers don't screw it up."

"Come on. Don't be a girl about it. We get shit done. You hear about that barrio captain who got killed last year? The Azteca up in Angeles. That was us. He was supposed to be impossible to get, but we got him." I leaned across the table and gave Nemesio a high-five.

"You didn't do that," Jonathan said.

"Sure we did. We know a few cops. Got one of their squad cars and pulled the guy over. Put him in cuffs, took him into the desert, and shot him." I omitted the part where Nemesio and I had nearly gotten ourselves killed trying to get out of the barrio with the captain, but whatever.

Jonathan was quiet, seemingly unimpressed.

"Hey," I said. "It's not like you're doing so great yourself. Heard you flipped out and killed Efren. What was that about?"

"That wasn't me."
"Not what people are saying."
"Well, it wasn't."
"Efren was Ing's guy."
"I know who Efren was."
"Word is there's a bounty on your head for that."
"I've heard."
"How about we go after Ing for you?"
Jonathan laughed. "Just get my money from BB."
"We could do both."
"My money."
"Call us if you change your mind," I said. "Hermanos de la Muerte."

VIII

The Boy

I'd gone to the abandoned mine in the mountains again. My grandma kept insisting I look around some more, but after a few hours of crawling through the dusty tunnels, I'd had enough and gave up.

I should've just asked Carlos if he had anything for me to do instead.

Half blinded by the sun and in a hurry to get on my bike, I almost walked into the giant hole, the old elevator shaft, that was outside the mine's entrance. My heel just barely caught the edge. Another inch and I would've been gone.

I leaned over the gap, checking out the rusted cage that'd snapped from the long-gone cables and wedged itself against the sides about as far down as the sunlight could reach. The fall would've probably broken an arm or leg. Or maybe I would've just ripped straight through the ancient metal like it was paper and kept on falling into the darkness.

There was a large rock nearby that could answer that question, so I grabbed it and tossed it in with a grunt. The weighty chunk landed with a deep boom, but the cage held firm. It didn't move, didn't slip, didn't come apart. Just sat there.

I looked for another rock, but the desert was mostly just sand and pebbles and shrubs that cascaded down the mountainside, so I left the cage alone and got on my bike, gunning it.

Down in the city, while I waited at a stoplight, Mozart started to play, and it took me a moment to realize it was the phone Carlos had given me. I dug it out of the compartment under the seat.

"Hey," he said. "Where are you? I need you to come over."

"Just down the road."

"Well, get back here."

"Sure." I tucked the phone away and raced off.

Carlos was sitting on his front steps. "Taking you to meet Ingeniero," he said as he got up and made his way to his Caprice.

I switched off the bike. "Who's that?"

"Someone you don't want to meet but have to." He smiled at me, then ducked into his car.

"What's that mean?" I asked after I'd gotten into the passenger side.

"Means he's a lunatic. But he's also the guy the Sinaloa Cartel put in charge of the city, so you do what he says. And today he wants to talk with you."

"Why? Am I in trouble?"

"The opposite actually. You're getting popular." He gave me another smile, then refused to answer another question. Near the city center, he pulled up to a two-story gray stucco house on Calle Ramon Aranda Poniente. "Just let him say what he wants to say, and we'll keep this short."

I nodded, and Carlos hopped out of the car.

We hadn't even gotten to the front door when it snapped open, and a man in a dark blue dress shirt, black jeans, and loafers appeared. He looked at Carlos, then at me, his eyes widening briefly behind rectangular glasses. "You *are* tall."

"Told you, Ingeniero," Carlos said.

"You did." The man waved his hand. "Please, come in." As we walked past, he asked, "How's Javier?"

"Javier's fine," Carlos said.

"He should be. Things have quieted." Ingeniero shut the door with a thud and made for the room to our right, a living room crowded with stacks of cardboard boxes.

I followed Carlos to the sofa in the middle of the mess. There was a coil hanging on the wall across from us that looked like a thick, braided rope, but after staring at it for a bit longer, I realized it wasn't a rope but a dried out snake. And its head had been chopped off. I leaned close to Carlos and pointed. "Is that thing—"

"Yep," he muttered.

"What's that?" Ingeniero asked as he moved an open box of books from an armchair.

"Nothing," Carlos said. "Lot of books."

Ingeniero took a seat and crossed his legs. "I'm cataloguing my collection. Finding some first editions I didn't even know I had."

"That's great." Carlos eyed the boxes around us.

Ingeniero pulled a book from a nearby box and held it up. "Bram Stoker's *Dracula*. You ever read this? It's very good." He smiled.

Carlos shook his head. I did the same.

"Well, if you ever want to borrow it, or any of these"—Ingeniero waved his hand around—"let me know. Just don't bend the pages. I'll kill you if you bend the pages."

I chuckled. Carlos didn't.

Ingeniero studied me for a second, then turned to Carlos. "What are you hearing about the Aztecas?"

Carlos straightened his back. "I guess they're loading up. But don't know what for."

"To be prepared," Ingeniero said. "You know what they're loading up on?"

"Guns."

Ingeniero smiled. "Specifically? AK-47s from what I hear."

Carlos scratched the back of his neck. "Yeah. Probably. There's a lot of them around for some reason."

"A shipment was stolen," Ingeniero told him. "I hope Javier is buying. They should be cheap."

Carlos shook his head. "No. He says money's tight."

"Will get tighter if he lets the competition keep 'loading up.'"

Carlos crossed his arms, then uncrossed them. "I know."

Ingeniero let the room get quiet.

A car with a bad engine drove by outside, backfiring once, and I jumped.

Ingeniero chuckled. "You taking care of this boy, Carlos?"

"Oh, for sure."

Ingeniero looked at me. "Is he?"

I nodded.

"Good. If the Aztecas start acting up, you stay close to Carlos. Do what he says. He'll keep you safe."

I nodded again.

"He'll keep your family safe too."

"I know."

"I know you do. That's why you're here, isn't it? Trying to keep the Moyas safe. Trying to do what Dad couldn't."

I didn't know what to say to that. I turned to Carlos for some help, but he only looked down at his lap.

Ingeniero pressed, "Dad was an army man, was he not?"

"Um." I bit my lip as my eyes went to my own lap.

"But that didn't end well, did it?"

I wrung my hands together. Looked at Ingeniero. The man smiled and raised his eyebrows in encouragement, so I went ahead and said, "No"

"What happened?"

"He was shot. Narcos shot him."

Ingeniero leaned back in his chair. "You know who exactly?"

I shook my head.

Ingeniero took off his glasses and waved them at Carlos, then himself. "We're narcos. Could've been us." He hung his glasses from the collar of his shirt and leaned forward. "Could've been me."

"It wasn't," I said.

"How would you know?" He smiled. "Tell me, what would you do...if I was the one who shot Castor, shot your dad?"

"I don't know."

"You know. What would you do?"

I was quiet.

Ingeniero got close enough that I could see a vein pulsing below his left eye. "Tell me."

I breathed deep, puffing out my chest. "I'd kill you."

"Precisely." Ingeniero pulled back and nodded his head hard. "Exactly." He pointed at me, and said to Carlos, "That's great, isn't it? He'd kill me."

Carlos gave a confused smirk. "Yeah?"

Ingeniero swatted my knee. "And if I knew you knew, I would've had Carlos take you out to the desert, not here. You understand?"

"I guess." I didn't.

"But we don't have to worry about that. It was the Aztecas who killed your dad. They were siphoning oil from a Pemex pipeline west of the city, and the army surprised them. They were all killed, including your dad's killer."

Ingeniero watched me for a moment. "Do you think your dad got one before he got his?"

"He got a medal," I quickly said.

"Hmm. A medal. Keep hanging around Carlos, and some army man will get a medal for killing you too."

I shook my head. "I'm helping my family."

"That's true. Everything we do is to help our families. So you keep it up. If the Aztecas start a fight with us, you fight back. To protect your family. You understand? And the Aztecas are not some junkie in the park."

"I know. I can fight."

Ingeniero sucked in his cheeks, then said, "I've got things quiet right now, but it can turn fast. You need to help if it comes to it. Whatever Carlos says, you do it. You help him. You help him, you help your family." Ingeniero put his glasses back on and got up. "Understood?"

I nodded several times. "Okay."

"Good." The man looked around the room. "I have work to tend to, so"—he turned to us and extended his hand—"if you don't mind."

Carlos said, "Nope," and jumped up from the couch, shaking Ingeniero's hand as he rose.

Ingeniero led us to the door, and just before we left, he said to Carlos, "I've got an issue in El Paso. Javier will tell you about. Get it handled, will you?"

"Absolutely," Carlos said as he hurried outside.

Ingeniero gave me a slap on the shoulder as I left. "Listen to Carlos. He'll watch over you. And your family."

~

Carlos and I sat at a stoplight, him drumming his fingers along the steering wheel, me thinking about my dad, the protector of our family (until he wasn't).

My mom had never told me what had happened. Nor my grandma.

They probably didn't know what had happened either, though. People didn't talk about the narcos. Even the newspapers didn't say much, only reporting on the basics, the facts, as if the violence was just a sporting event with a box score.

Two men had been murdered.
Ages twenty and twenty-one.
Four bullets hit one, seven hit the other.
The attack had happened outside an elementary school (or outside a Superette).

And that was it. No names, no reasons, no accusations, no justice.

Nobody talked. We all just moved on.

Someday, my family would move on, literally. Maybe back to Michoacán, where my grandparents had lived as subsistence farmers. They'd come here in anticipation of the signing of NAFTA, after the government had promised city jobs and city money from the maquiladoras that would be built in Juárez. Except my family, like most of the city's population, still had little to nothing. Those in the Anapra barrio didn't even have electricity or fresh water.

NAFTA was bullshit. Michoacán had been a million times better.

And a million times safer.

So someday, when my family could manage it, we'd leave.

Carlos rolled through the intersection, but instead of heading back to Joaquín Terrazas, he took us to a dusty, crumbling box of a house on Calle Durazno.

"Who's here?" I asked. The place looked like a thick-headed troll with barred-up windows on each side of a wide door and a cracked set of frowning steps.

"Javier," Carlos said. "He's got some work for us."

"What kind of work?"

"You don't need the money?"

"Just asking." I got out before Carlos changed his mind about us being there.

We marched across a sandy strip of front lawn to the sad, ashen-faced troll house. Carlos didn't knock. He just went right in, and I followed.

The front room was pretty much empty. Three men were sitting on a dirty, ripped blue sofa off to the right, their faces changing colors in the light of the TV in the corner.

Carlos asked, "He ready?"

"All yours," one of them said, not bothering to even turn around to look at us.

Carlos led me into a hallway to a bedroom, where a man was sitting on a flimsy wooden chair, his mouth taped over, his hands and feet bound. Carlos stepped to the side. "So," he said, giving me a smile, "we need to rough this guy up a little."

The place smelled of blood and sweat.

I looked at the man who seemed plenty roughed up already with cuts across his face and a welt above his eye. His shirt had been torn and stretched, and his right foot was missing its shoe, the sock wet and dangling from his toes.

Carlos slapped me on the back. "Don't hold back like you did with JP."

"Don't hold back?"

"Like you did at the park."

"Okay." I didn't think I had.

Carlos stepped close. "We need to keep things safe. Keep things in order. So don't hold back. This needs to send the right message."

Two of the men that'd been watching TV stood in the doorway.

"Let him really have it," Carlos said, punching the air a couple of times.

"Show us what you got," one of the men said.

I nodded sharply, then went to the bound man, the sour smell intensifying. He wasn't looking at me. Or any of us. His chin just rested on his chest, so I grabbed him by his armpits and lifted him to his feet. "Hey," I said.

The man kept his head bowed. I hit him in the stomach, just trying to get his attention, but he buckled over and threw up.

I jumped back.

"Keep going," Carlos yelled.

"Nail him," the second guy in the doorway added.

So I stepped forward, pushed the man back into the chair, and let him have it, eventually just closing my eyes and punching, punching, punching.

When Carlos finally stepped in, the man was a mewling mess, blood dribbling from his nose and split eyebrows. Spit bubbles growing and popping between his lips. Carlos pushed the man's forehead, sending his head lolling around.

"Nice job." Carlos patted me on the shoulder. "Let's go get something to eat." He turned to the men in the doorway. "You hungry?"

They shook their heads. "Nah."

Carlos escorted me from the room.

As we headed for the front door, the man who'd remained on the couch watching TV said, "Where you headed?"

"Get some food," Carlos said.

The man turned from the TV and looked at Carlos. He had the face of a bulldog.

"You want us to get you something, Javier?"

"Maybe." Javier stood from the couch, straightening his button-down shirt with a quick, hard tug. He turned and stared at me. "Or maybe I'll just go with."

~

Carlos drove us to a small chicken and hamburger spot a few blocks away. Before we went in, Javier finally stopped eyeing me and pointed at a monument of Emiliano Zapata across the street. "You know who that is?"

"Zapata," I answered.

"Damn right it is. I fucking love that guy."

Zapata stood on a pedestal, holding a document in his left hand and a shotgun aimed and ready in his right. He'd originally faced north, but the mayor of Juárez declared it in bad taste to let Zapata point his gun toward El Paso, so he had the monument turned. Zapata now pointed his gun at our barrio.

"Such a badass," Javier said, grabbing the door to the restaurant.

We found an empty booth near the back, ignoring the counter where people were supposed to place their orders. Javier just waved his hand at one of the girls, and she brought over a pitcher of horchata.

"Have some," he said to me after pouring himself a glass. He then glared across the table at Carlos. "So mijo, talk to me. What'd Ing say?"

"He likes him."

Javier's beady dog eyes shifted to me as I was filling a glass with horchata. "Is Ing worried?"

"About him?"

"No, the Aztecas."

I set the pitcher back on the table and sipped my drink, pretending not to notice Javier's stare.

"I don't think so," Carlos said. "I am, though."

Javier pushed back from the table, sitting up straight. He looked at Carlos. "Why?"

Carlos took the pitcher. "They're loading up."

"So?" Javier said. "You scared, mijo?"

"We're not in a good spot."

Javier let out a burst of laughter, then took a long drink of his horchata. "This stuff is the best. I love it. Zapata loved it too."

"Guys are trying to get cheap on us," Carlos said.

"Like BB. He hasn't paid in forever."

"Go get the fucker."

"He's been lying low."

"Put the word out. Someone'll rat on him."

Carlos nodded. "Maybe, but what I'm saying is that people think we're getting soft. JP tried to knife him the other day."

"Who? BB? So?"

Carlos jutted his thumb at me.

"Ha. Welcome to the club." Javier leaned on the table. "So what's your story?" he asked me.

"My story?"

"Yeah. Like how'd you get so fucking big, niño? You're huge," Javier laughed.

I tried to smile, not really sure if that was a compliment, though. "I don't know."

"Carlos says you've been doing some work for us."

"Trying to help, yeah."

"Is he?" Javier turned to Carlos.

"He is," Carlos said, nodding.

Javier came back to me. "You like getting paid?"

"Yeah. I need it."

Javier grinned wide. "You need it? For what? You got a little girlfriend?" Javier snickered to himself, then before I could answer, said to Carlos, "You remember Evaristo's girl? That pinche loudmouth?"

"Oh yeah."

Javier shook his head, examined his horchata for a moment, then glared at me. "She wouldn't keep quiet, niño. Always talking, talking, talking. You make sure your girl knows how to keep quiet about things, okay?"

I nodded. "Sure."

"Evaristo's girl thought it was so cool how tough her boyfriend was. She loved telling everyone. Problem is, niño"—Javier leaned even farther across the table—"if you tell people, you put us in a bad spot. It's not good for us." He leaned back in his seat. "So keep your fucking mouth shut."

"I will."

"I know you will," Javier said, "or I'll make Evaristo put a bullet in your head too."

I looked from Javier to Carlos, then back.

Javier gave me a wink before saying to Carlos, "Ing tell you about the problem in El Paso? About that bitch trafficker?"

"He mentioned it," Carlos said.

"Trafficker killed Efren."

"Why?"

"He's trying to move kids now." Javier gulped the last of his horchata. "We've got to shut that down. Have to bring the bitch back here." Javier gestured at me. "You help get him."

"In El Paso?" I asked. "I don't have a passport."

Javier gave a snort. "You think that matters?"

"No?" I guessed as the girl who'd brought the horchata returned with cheeseburgers and fries.

Carlos grabbed his burger and bit into it. "What's Ingeniero's going to do with the guy?"

"Something fucked up," Javier said, bits of fry flying from his mouth.

"I mean, will we have to take him back to El Paso when he's done with him?"

"No chance. The guy's a dead man." Javier drank the last of the horchata straight from the pitcher, then got out of the booth and walked to the back of the restaurant, disappearing into the bathroom.

I looked at Carlos. "I'm really going to El Paso?"

"Yeah. Congratulations. This is big money."

"And I don't need a passport?"

"Nope. But anyway, don't ask questions. Just go along with it. You want money for your family, don't you?"

"Of course."

"This will get you like a grand or something, so just

be quiet."

"A grand? No way."

"At least."

"That's crazy."

"Well, it won't be like some walk in the park. It's serious business now."

But a grand, I thought.

~

It was dusk, and the sand and dust that the afternoon winds had picked up out in the desert had settled, coating the city. As we went from the car to the Durazno house, we left a trail of footprints in our wake.

"String him up, string him up, string him up," Javier was mumbling to himself. He opened the front door and paused, staring at the two guys we'd left behind who were now slouched on the couch. "Hey. Dante. Evaristo. Off your asses. Chop, chop."

They both got up, not too fast but not all that slow either, and the five of us went to the back room, where the man Carlos had asked me to beat up was still sitting.

The guy raised his head, but I doubted he could see anything. His eyes were swollen to little slits and covered in crusty blood.

A white sheet had been spread out on the floor and spray painted with a message, but before I could get a good look at it, Carlos picked it up and wadded it into a ball. "Dante," he said, and tossed it to one of the men who looked like a thinner, greasier version of himself. Carlos turned to Javier, who had knelt beside the man in the chair. "He good to go?"

"Maybe." Javier got in close to the man's face, inspecting him, tilting his head side to side. He blew a puff of air and watched the man flinch. He chuckled. "See ya later, bitch," he whispered before stepping back. "Yeah, he's good to go."

Carlos flicked open a utility knife he'd drawn from his pocket and cut the tape around the man's ankles. "Taking you home," he said while he did it. He slapped the man on each ankle, getting him to separate his feet. "Now up."

The man struggled and wobbled.

"Up," Javier shouted.

When the man still couldn't get to his feet, Carlos grabbed him by the armpit. I swooped in and grabbed the other, and we lifted the wilted man stinking of sweat and blood from the chair.

"Bag him," Javier said.

Dante laughed. "The guy can't see shit."

"Bag him," Javier growled.

Dante's smile dropped. He turned to the guy beside him. "You got one, Evaristo?"

"I'll check." The guy disappeared into the hallway. "Got this," he called out, returning with a blindfold.

"Good enough," Javier said.

Evaristo tied the blindfold around the man's head.

"March," Javier said, and Carlos and I went in lockstep with the man out of the room to the backyard, where there was a black Ford Lobo parked in the dirt.

Dante climbed into the back and helped guide the man up into the truck beside him.

"Now you," Carlos said to me, so I squeezed in as well. "Where's Angel?" Carlos asked as he stepped away from the Lobo.

"Right there," Dante said, pointing at some guy hurrying from the house with a bundle of rope in his hand. "Been on the crapper for the last two hours."

"I couldn't help it," Angel said as he climbed into the front passenger seat. "Fucking McDonald's."

Javier stepped close to Angel, laughing. "Told you about those Buffalo Blasts. Boom!"

"Whatever." Angel shut his door.

As Evaristo got behind the wheel, Carlos leaned in and said to me, "Just do what these guys say."

"This the newbie?" Angel glanced over his shoulder and looked me up and down. "Christ, kid, how tall are you?"

Carlos slapped me on the knee. "He eats his veggies."

Angel chuckled, facing forward again. "Guess so."

Carlos stepped back and gave me a stern look. "You listen to them, okay?" After I'd nodded, he said, "Good," and shut the door. He and Javier then headed back into the house.

Evaristo started the truck and rolled it through the dirt yard and onto the street. Everyone kept quiet, even the blindfolded man, whose breathing had grown steady and calm. After we'd gone a half mile or so, Evaristo stopped in the middle of the Azucenas overpass, a little span over a dry viaduct.

"Hold it," Evaristo said, watching as a white truck approached. His hand dropped to his lap, where his shirt was lifted slightly and the glint of black metal hid underneath.

Dante had his hands in his lap too. I couldn't see what Angel was doing, but I assumed they all had a gun. It was probably just me (and our captive) who didn't.

The truck passed, though, and it didn't matter.

Doors flew open, and Dante said, "We're home." He started pulling the man from the truck, so I helped push from the other side.

Angel grabbed his rope and hurried around the front.

Evaristo walked up to the overpass railing, leaned over it, and said, "Perfect." He took one end of the rope from Angel and wrapped it around the rail as Angel held onto the other end, twisting and knotting it in his hands.

Dante and I led the man from the truck, shuffling

along to the railing.

"Home sweet home," Dante said.

The bridge, and the streets around it, were quiet. A mechanic's shop surrounded by disassembled vehicles watched from one side, while a brick apartment building speckled with glowing windows stared from the other.

I kept my head low.

Angel gave the rope a tug, then lifted the knot, a noose, into the air.

Dante nudged the man under it.

My hands were on the man's neck, and I could feel his muscles stiffen as Angel dropped the noose over his head.

I let go, so the knot could fall into place, but that was a mistake. The man shook and twisted and bounced around.

"Grab him," Angel shouted. "Flip him. Fast."

But the man slipped away.

"Shit. Shit," Dante (or Angel, or both) cried out.

I knelt down to grab the man's legs, figuring if I held his legs, that'd give the others time to wrestle him under control, but before I even touch the man, his knee caught me on the side of the head, knocking me back on my ass.

"Shit, shit, shit," someone was saying as I blinked and fumbled around on the pavement.

I tried to stand, but the world was spinning, and I fell against the Lobo. I stared at its giant wheel, trying to focus on just one specific lug nut. Off to the side, some massive white figure rumbled up to the front of the Lobo. I blinked once, twice, and turned my head. I called out to the others, but they didn't hear.

The white truck from earlier had come back, and its doors were swinging open.

I called out again, yelling, "Dante."

Two men dropped from the truck and lifted their

guns.

"Dante!"

The men weren't aiming at me; they were facing the railing.

I tried to stand, grabbed the truck's fender, but my vision swirled, my hands slipped, and I hit the ground.

The men, the Aztecas (who else could they be?) opened fired, and as the gunshots rang out, I went scurrying, crawling, rolling under the Lobo.

The Aztecas never saw me. I kept wiggling across the pavement and slipped out the other side.

Dante and the others had drawn their guns and were now firing back.

I could've maybe run. I don't know. I didn't really think about it. Instead, I got up, lowered my head, and bull-rushed the Aztecas.

I hit the one nearest to me, the driver, a small man with a gold necklace that broke apart when I leveled him with a shoulder to the chest. He went rolling, tumbling over himself, gold links scattering, sparkling in the light of the street lamps.

I rushed him again, head down, and just as he was getting to his feet, I hit him, lifting him, driving him, carrying him on my shoulder across the overpass, crying out as I did it. I only stopped when I slammed the man against the far railing.

It didn't take much to flip him over. I let go, a second passed, and the Azteca hit the concrete headfirst, popping like some fat desert spider.

I took a breath, leaned over the railing, and tried to let my thoughts catch up with what had just happened. The wind was making a whistling sound as it passed under the bridge, and I realized that that was all there was to hear.

I turned around, and the gunfight was over.

The other Azteca was on his back between the trucks in a pool of blood. The blindfolded man was slumped against the railing, the noose still around his neck, a bunch of widening dark spots on his chest. Evaristo was grimacing, clutching a bloody thigh, limping towards the Lobo.

I ran to help him get into the back of the truck. The sheet that we'd brought with us was crumpled on the floor, so I grabbed it and wrapped it around his thigh, tightening it until he screamed.

"You'll be okay," I said. "You will."

Dante called out, "Get over here," and when I turned around, he said it again.

Angel was sprawled on the ground, not moving, and Dante was trying to lift him. I went over to give him a hand, but I stopped when I got close. Angel had a weakening stream of blood coming from a hole in his neck. "Is he dead?"

"Not leaving him," Dante shouted. "Pick him up." He wrapped his arms around Angel's wet chest. "Pick him up."

I grabbed Angel's legs, and we put him beside Evaristo. Dante slammed the door, and Angel's head bumped against the window, marking the glass with a greasy, red smear.

"Get in," Dante ordered as he jumped behind the wheel.

I scanned the overpass from the apartment building to the mechanic's shop. It was empty. One more thing needed to be done, though. We'd gone through enough shit already, and we couldn't leave now, so I sprinted over to the blindfolded man and flipped him over the rail. The rope tied to the rail snapped tight a second later.

"Let's go," Dante yelled.

"I know." I raced back to the truck, and Dante stomped on the gas.

He flipped a phone into my lap.

"What's this for?" I asked.

"Message Doc K. Tell him we're coming." Dante

swung the truck around a corner. "Tell Carlos to head to the hospital too."

I did as he asked, and then just held on as Dante raced through the streets, squeezing between traffic and blasting through intersections. When we reached the hospital, there were three nurses outside waiting for us.

I helped them get Evaristo into a wheelchair, making sure to take back the bloody sheet with whatever was written on it.

Another nurse came out and was checking on Angel. He started to say something, but Dante cut him off. "We weren't leaving him. Put him wherever you put them." After the nurse took Angel away, Dante and I stood looking down at our shoes. "Just sucks," Dante mumbled.

I nodded, then looked around, scanning the dirt parking lot across the street, checking for white trucks. The sun had completely set, and the lot had no lights, so it was hard to see. "Is this hospital good?" I asked.

Dante massaged his neck and leaned against the truck. "What do you mean 'good'?"

I gestured at the entrance to the single-story building. "My grandma won't bring us here."

"Probably because she thinks it's a narco hospital."

"Is it?"

"Yeah."

Our clothes were streaked with dirt and blood.

"I don't think I can go home like this. My grandma would kill me."

Dante snorted.

"I'm serious."

"I know. That's why it's funny."

I picked at my shirt.

"Just tell her you were having some fun. Tell her you were playing luchador and flipping people over the ropes."

I grimaced. "That won't work."

"It was a joke," Dante said. "Come on. Maybe there's a shirt back at the house."

~

When we got to Durazno, Javier was spread out on the couch playing a video game. "Have a beer," he said as we walked in.

I pretended not to hear the offer. My dad had once given me a taste of his beer during a celebration for busting up some big drug shipment, and I still hadn't gotten over the rancid taste of it. I dropped the bloodied sheet Dante had asked me to bring inside on the floor.

Javier looked at me, then went back to smashing his fingers on the controller. "Waste of a good narco note."

"It kept Evaristo from bleeding out," Dante said as he disappeared down the hallway.

I sat on the couch, inspecting my hands and the blood that had started to dry and crack around my knuckles and fingernails.

Dante returned with a towel. "Move over," he told Javier before plopping down on the couch between us. He finished wiping off his arms, then handed me the damp towel. While I cleaned up, he grabbed two beers from the case next to Javier's feet and pushed one in my direction. "Here you go."

"I'm okay," I said.

"After all that shit, you don't want a drink?"

I shook my head, pretending to focus on a stubborn spot of blood. "No. Not really."

"Just take it."

"But I don't want it."

Javier laughed. "'But I don't want it.'"

"It's gross."

Dante kept the bottle hanging between us. "It's just beer."

My hands and arms were clean. I was just rubbing at nothing now.

"Have a drink." Dante grabbed the towel from my hands and flicked it aside.

For some reason, I thought it'd help by saying, "I'm not supposed to drink. It's the law," but Dante looked at me like I was stupid.

"The law?" he said.

"I'm not old enough to drink."

"Yeah, Carlos told us. You're thirteen. I don't care."

"I don't want it."

Dante's hand (and the bottle) dropped to his lap.

Javier paused the video game and tossed aside the controller. He reached around the couch, grabbed a bottle of tequila, and showed me the label. "You don't want a beer, then you're getting this: Volcan De Mi Tierra. We're all having a drink." He pulled the cork and took a swig, then shoved the bottle into my hands. "Drink," he said.

Dante lifted his beer to me. "Salud, you little beast."

I couldn't keep saying no, and for all I knew, the tequila was better than the beer, so I lifted the bottle and with both of them watching, I tipped it back and swallowed.

I thought I had passed the test.

It didn't taste like anything.

But then I took a breath, and the burn erupted everywhere. "Jesus." I leaned forward, choking, holding the bottle out, pushing it away, hoping one of them would take it.

Javier only erupted with laughter.

"Here," Dante said. "Chase it down with this."

I turned my head slightly. The beer bottle was right there in my face.

"It helps," he said.

I sat up, grabbed the beer, and hoped he was telling the truth. He was, and I sighed and sank into the couch.

Javier's phone chimed with a message. He read it.

"So Angel's dead, huh?"

"Kind of a shit show," Dante said.

Javier looked over at me. "How about another drink for Angel?"

"Please, no."

He laughed. "Whatever."

Dante gave me a swat on the leg. "You should've seen this guy, though, Javier. What a beast."

"What'd he do?" Javier picked up his controller and went back to his game.

"Bum-rushed the Aztecas. Head down. Full speed. Flipped him right over the damn rail." Dante turned to me. "Do you even have a gun? You don't, do you?"

"Nobody gave me one."

"You're a beast."

Javier started laughing. "He's a fucking idiot."

Dante hit me on the leg again. "Nah. That was pretty badass. I'll get you a gun, though." He hopped off the couch and started down the hall.

I got up to follow, but Javier held up his hand, saying, "You just stay here," so I sat back down and watched him die a few times in the video game.

When Dante returned, he said, "We've got nothing here."

"Why would we?" Javier grumbled.

"I'll get you one tomorrow or something. Found this." Dante tossed me a blue shirt.

It didn't smell clean, but it wasn't splashed with blood either, so I switched shirts. The new one only covered half my stomach.

Dante smirked. "Hey, that's all I got." He grabbed his beer and sat.

I tried stretching the shirt, tugging it, but all I did was break a few threads.

Carlos stepped through the front door and paused, giving me a cock-eyed look.

Before he could say anything, Javier spoke up. "We good?"

Carlos looked at Javier, then back at me. "Why're you—"

"We good?" Javier barked.

"Yeah," Carlos said. "We're good. Just got muscle." He came over beside the couch. "Why're you wearing a kid's shirt? Did Dante make you wear this?"

"Absolutely not. And that's an *adult* medium," Dante said. "The kid's just a beast. Thirteen years old. God damn."

Carlos pointed at the white sheet on the floor. "Why didn't you hang it?"

"You want Evaristo to die, or you want us to hang it?" Dante grabbed his beer and took a sip.

Carlos scratched the back of his head. "Okay. Can you still read it?"

"Don't know. Take a look."

Carlos unfurled the sheet. We all read it.

> *This is what happens to the asshole police who take sides with the Aztecas. Don't fuck with us.*
> *Yours truly, AA.*

"Assholes," Dante said, sipping the beer.

"Was that guy a cop?" I asked.

Carlos nodded. "But he was La Línea, so—"

"Corrupt fuckers," Javier said as he mashed the controller's buttons.

I scooted a little closer to the edge of the couch. "We killed a cop?"

"Absolutely not," Dante said. "We beat one up. Actually, *you* beat one up. The Aztecas killed him."

"Don't worry about it," Carlos said, letting the sheet fall to the floor. "We all make our choices. He made his."

IX

The Boy

Carlos eventually took me back home, but instead of going inside, I got on my bike and rode around, just wandering in the dark, turning whenever I saw a truck, white or not, coming my way.

At some point, I came up on an electronics store and found a distraction in the glow of the TVs shining through the barred windows. I parked and stared, mesmerized by the collection of cartoons, sitcoms, soap operas, and sports games.

My hand settled atop the pocket where I'd put a fresh one hundred dollars, another payment from Carlos. This much cash would cover an entire month's supply of insulin.

I probably had enough for two months' worth.

Maybe I could spend a little.

This was more money than my mom could make in a year at the maquiladora. And if Javier sent me to El Paso like he said he would, and if he gave me a thousand dollars like Carlos said he would…

What was I worrying about anymore?

And a TV would be such a cool gift. An early birthday present for Katie and myself. I climbed off my bike and went in.

When I got home, I set the twenty-four-inch Sony Trinitron on the floor and waited for the applause. But the room was quiet.

I peeked around the side of the couch. Isa was curled up there, looking sick.

"Hey. You okay?" I asked.

"Head hurts."

"Your BG high?" I knelt next to her.

She nodded. "I was low and had some juice."

"Too much juice?"

She squeezed her eyes tight.

"You want to take some insulin?"

"I took some. I can't take more."

I sat on the floor and rubbed her back. "You take whatever you need. It's okay."

"Have to wait."

The front door opened, and my mom came in, pausing in the doorway. "What's this?"

"Oh, I got that"—a grin formed—"for our birthdays."

"You found this? Where?"

"No. I bought it. I, uh, helped Carlos move some stuff. He gave me a hundred dollars."

"A *hundred* dollars?"

"It was really heavy stuff." I stood up, arching my back like it needed a good stretch.

"Mijo," my mom sighed. "This is very thoughtful of you, but there's a lot of things we need before a TV."

My grandma emerged from the kitchen. "You helped *who*? Carlos? The neighbor?"

Katie came up behind her, peeking into the living room. "A TV," she squealed, and ran to the box, tugging at the flaps.

My grandma hurried across the room after here. "No, no, no." She pulled Katie away from the box. "This goes back."

"Why?" Katie groaned.

Isa tried to lift herself over the back of the couch for a look. "A TV?"

My mom took one look at her. "You're high, aren't you, Isa?"

My sister slid back onto the couch, eyes closed. "Yeah."

"What's Isa's BG?" my mom asked my grandma.

"I don't know. I've been making supper. She didn't tell me she was feeling bad."

"She shouldn't have to tell you, Mom."

"I can make dinner, or I can monitor her blood sugar. Not both."

My mom ignored her and grabbed Isa's glucose meter off the floor near the couch.

"No," Isa whined. "There's only three left."

"We need to know your BG. Especially when you're feeling like this." She took one of Isa's fingers and pricked it with the lancet, then gave it a small squeeze and touched the droplet to the test strip.

"I'll get you more strips," I told Isa.

"How much insulin did you give yourself?" my mom asked as the meter flashed 475.

"Two," Isa told her.

"When?"

"Hour ago."

"You need more. Much more."

"No," Isa complained.

"Hija preciosa," she whispered. "You need it." My mom looked at me and clucked her tongue, the signal to go get the insulin and a syringe from the kitchen, so I hurried around the corner.

"Pozole's burning," I said when I came back, handing the insulin and syringe to my mom.

"Shit on a shingle," my grandma said as she scuttled away.

Katie, now free of her grasp, dove at the box, tearing it open. "TV, TV, TV..."

X

The Boy

I didn't return to the car wash near the roundabout, sell paletas near the border, or scavenge around the mine anymore. I didn't want to miss out on anything, so I just started hanging out at the house on Durazno.

Not much happened, though. We went out once, but that was just to attend the prayer vigil for Angel. His family had it at their house. They laid his body atop their kitchen table and draped him in a clean, white sheet, then surrounded him with lilies. Carlos and the others left a small bit of cash for his family, so I did the same. Angel's family didn't seem to appreciate that we were there, though, so we eventually left and went back to the house to play video games.

The gun Dante had promised me arrived a day later, and that was cool. It was a black 9mm Beretta Centerfire.

"Looks nice," I said when Dante handed it to me.

"Looks nice, 'cause it is nice."

I put my hand around the grip, squeezing the textured rubber. It was a little smaller and a little lighter than I remembered, but I'd grown since I'd last held a Beretta, so I guess I should've expected that. "How much was this?"

"Was a favor owed to me. Don't worry about it. You want to try it out? Make sure it actually works?"

"You don't think it does?"

"Well, let me ask you this: do you want to find out now, or when someone's pointing a gun at you?"

"Now," I said. "Now."

"Then come on. I got a place we can go. Curious to see what kind of shot you are anyway."

"I'm pretty good."

Dante laughed. "Sure, you are."

I didn't need to convince him. I just tucked the gun into my waistband, and walked out with him to the Lobo.

When we passed by the Ciudad Juárez Cathedral and its plaza filled with people and food carts and vendors, Dante asked if I remembered what the place used to look like.

"No. What?"

"You seriously don't remember?"

"No. But can we stop?" I asked. "I want to get something." After Dante had pulled to the curb, I pointed at one of the vendors with a row of yellow buckets filled with spices and herbs. "My grandma needs some ancho chiles."

"Aren't you the good grandson?" Dante scanned the crowd. "Just hurry."

So I did, hopping out of the truck, rushing up to the vendor, then darting back.

"I know why you don't remember," Dante said as he drove away. "You're too young. This was probably ten years ago, but that place used to be a shithole. The whole thing was falling apart. People wouldn't go near it 'cause bricks were coming loose from the towers."

"Good thing they it up."

"You know who fixed it up?"

"Who?"

"The Sinaloa Cartel. Paid for the whole restoration."

"Nice of them."

Dante nodded. "It was. Those were the good days. Now they're just barely holding on, and we're having to fight for everything every day."

"Sinaloa's rich, though, aren't they?"

"Not like they used to be. They're losing territory. Losing routes."

"Who's taking it?"

"The Juárez Cartel. Them and their bitch Aztecas. You don't know that?"

I shook my head. I had no clue about any of it.

Something I *did* know was that the Periférica Camino Real Highway we were now driving on had once been part of the longest trade route in the world, going from the center of Mexico all the way up to New Mexico. I could've told Dante about that. I had learned about the road in school (maybe Katie was learning about it now), and I'd felt proud when I could recite the story of the road to the class, but as I thought about it now, that bit of knowledge didn't seem all that impressive anymore. It just felt a little pointless, so I kept quiet.

Dante followed the highway up into the hills, then turned off onto a dirt road that curled around the Cristo de Curiel, a giant statue of Christ that watched over the city. We continued west through the desert for another five or ten minutes before stopping.

"Here we be," Dante said when we'd both hopped out of the truck. "This way." He walked off into the desert, and I followed, weaving around boulders topped with fat, sunbathing spiny lizards and between scrub bushes. Eventually, we came upon a waterless gully and descended into it.

"Welcome to Dante's Firing Range." He pointed at the opposite embankment where there were several road signs jammed into the earth, each pitted with a random scattering of holes.

"Cool." I checked the Beretta's clip and picked out a malformed stop sign.

"Don't go crazy. Just shoot a couple times. Get the feel for it. Make sure it's working. We don't want to waste ammo. Shit's not cheap."

"Okay." I steadied myself, then I put two bullets right through the O.

"Damn," Dante muttered.

"Told you."

"You *can* shoot."

It wasn't the first time I'd fired a gun. That had been when I was six years old. My dad had taken me. He'd wrapped his arms around me, held me steady, put his fingers over mine, and pulled the trigger. We'd had a few more times at the range before he died.

"Watch this," Dante said, drawing a pistol from under his shirt. "Watch the pedestrian crossing sign." He squeezed off a couple of shots, and the sign went untouched. "Well, you don't really need to be too accurate." He quickly pulled the trigger five more times, hitting nothing but sand. "Just being fast is good too."

I nodded and fired at the stop sign again, hitting it over and over.

"Yeah, fuck you too."

I turned to Dante's sign and put a bullet in the head of one of the pedestrians.

"Okay. Range time is over," Dante said. "Quite wasting bullets."

"Yeah, sure." I set the safety back in place.

"You know what I like?" Dante asked, tucking his gun away. "Grenades. You ever use a grenade?"

"No. Do you have one?'

"Ran out a couple months ago, but those are cool. Expensive, but worth it. They'll clear a room no problem. Pull the pin, toss it, everyone goes down. Fuck being accurate." Dante took out his phone and read a message. "We should go." He looked up at me. "Javier's got a job for us."

~

As we drove into the outer barrios of the city, Dante was saying, "Javier really needs to stop using these guys. This is like the third or fourth time they've done this."

"Done what?" I asked.

"Hit the wrong house. Dumb fucks."

"What's Javier want us to do?"

"Get his money back."

"How much?"

"Three grand."

"Do you think he'll give us some? Like a reward?"

"We'll find out, won't we?"

I couldn't hold back my grin. And I was still grinning when Dante pulled up to a sagging house scarred with patches of exposed wire mesh. I threw open my door.

"Hold on," Dante said. "Just wait." He got out and came around the truck. "They're dumb fucks, but we still have to be careful."

"Sure." I let Dante pass, then fell in lockstep behind him.

A fence made of wooden pallets and scrap metal surrounded the house, and Dante nudged the rusty box spring that acted as a gate. At the front door, I pulled out my gun and started to tap the barrel of it against my hip.

Dante looked at me, looked at the Beretta, tap, tap, tapping. "Just be cool."

I nodded—"I'm cool"—but I didn't stop.

"Whatever." He knocked and someone inside yelled

to come in. Dante tried the knob and it turned. He gave the door a gentle push, letting it swing open until it bumped against the inside wall. We stayed where we were. "Yo. It's Dante."

"Hey, man," someone replied back. "Who you got with you?"

"A friend."

I leaned over Dante's shoulder and peeked inside. The place was a bit like my house (a living room, a kitchen in the back, a bedroom off to the right), but it was a dump, wrappers and food cartons and empty bottles and crumpled cans everywhere. Three men were spread out on a beaten leather couch in the midst of the mess, their feet half buried in trash.

"Get in. Shut the door," the one in the middle complained. "It's hot out."

Dante glanced around, inspecting the doorframe, inspecting the room. "Yeah. Okay," he finally said.

The carpet made a crunching sound as we stepped in. I shut the door, and the men on the couch went back to their TV that was pushed against the wall to our right. The window behind it was covered with a sheet, and dried chunks of food or vomit or maybe something worse was splattered across the still fabric.

"Don't you have any lights in here?" Dante asked, flicking a switch on the wall but getting nothing for the effort. We both looked up and saw that all the bulbs had either died or been smashed, their sharp edges poking from their sockets.

"We like it dark," the middle man said.

The man on his left folded his hands across his pudgy belly, pulled his feet from the garbage, and rested them on a stack of wooden crates, knocking aside an empty soda cup from a Pemex station in the process.

"Javier sent us to pick up his money," Dante said.

"Yep, yep," the man in the middle, a wiry twenty-something guy I could easily take down, said. He rocked himself forward and stood up with a jerk, nearly tipping over the crates. After giving himself a moment to get steady, he said, "It's in the kitchen," then shuffled around the couch, kicking garbage as his feet dragged through the filth.

"Watch them," Dante told me as he followed the guy into the back room.

I took a step closer to the couch, checking for a gun or a knife, but there was just a razor on a piece of glass atop the crates. Something had been crushed into a bluish powder and scraped into a pile.

The pudgy guy squinted at me. "We went to the address Javier gave us. Not right you taking the money back." He dropped his feet and pulled himself upright, scooting to the edge of the couch, leaning over the crates. "Not our fault." He started to reach for the razor.

"Leave that alone," I said.

"Chill. I'm coming down," he grumbled. "I need a bump. You mind?"

"Later," I said.

"Fuck you, 'later'."

"Just sit. Don't do anything."

"No. I'm having a fucking bump."

The third man, a guy about as skinny as the one who led Dante into the kitchen, came out of his stupor and said, "Come on. Let him have it."

"Just wait until we're gone," I said.

"I'm taking a bump. I don't care." Pudgy reached for the razor again.

"Don't touch it."

He ignored me, saying, "Javier's lucky he's got us. Not many people would shoot a bunch of women like that. Not for three thousand. No way."

"You shot some women?"

The third man said, "Half a dozen or so."

"Don't forget the babies." Pudgy snorted a long line of the blue powder.

"Babies?" I said.

"It was a baby shower," the third man said.

My eyes went wide. "You shot up a baby shower? How could you do that?"

Pudgy snickered and wiped his nose. "Well, drugs always help."

"Hey," the other guy said. "We were just following orders. That was the address Javier gave us."

Pudgy nodded. "And Javier said, 'Shoot everyone there,' so that's what we did."

"You're joking," I said, shaking my head. "You didn't shoot up a baby shower."

Pudgy pointed across the room. "That look like a joke, man?"

Several pink gift-wrapped packages with colorful bows and ribbons were piled against the side of the TV.

Pudgy got up with a groan, walked over to the gifts, and picked one up. "What do you think we got in here?" He shook the box, then tore the wrap away. "Bootees! But not my size." He dropped the little knit bootees to the floor and picked up another box that had a streak of blood down its neatly creased fold. "Not our fault," he said before tearing into it.

I was tapping the Beretta against my thigh. "How many women were there?"

Pudgy inspected the second gift, a fluffy blanket, then rubbed it against his cheek. "Maybe eight or nine. Does the pregnant lady count as two?" He laughed.

I turned toward the kitchen. "Dante?" It came out as barely a whisper. "Dante?" I stepped around the couch, kicking garbage out of my way, hurrying to the back of the house. I then froze.

Dante and the wiry man were in the middle of the kitchen, their guns drawn and aimed at each other's head.

Dante looked at me, then back at the man. "Serafin's decided he doesn't want to give us the money, and that's fine. We're leaving."

"Yeah. Because that's what's fair," the man, Serafin, hissed. He eyed a roll of cash wrapped with a rubber band on the counter. "That's ours."

"Yep. All yours," Dante said.

I checked behind me. Pudgy tore open another gift while the man on the couch watched, both of them oblivious.

"We're going," Dante told Serafin. "Okay? Be cool."

"Go," Serafin said, flicking the gun toward the front of the house.

"We're going. I'm lowering my gun, and we're going."

"Do it, then."

Dante's gun went to his side, and he took a slow step back toward me. "We're going."

I moved out of the kitchen, out of Serafin's sight.

On the other side of the room, Pudgy dropped the last of the gifts to the floor and stumbled back onto the couch. "Junk's worthless. Where's the Walkman and shit?" He leaned over the table and went for his line of powder again, asking the other man, "You want one?"

I pressed against the wall that separated the kitchen and the living room, nearly knocking a painting from its hook. Santa Muerte, the saint of death, glared at me through her white veil.

Dante came backstepping out of the kitchen.

Pudgy let out an excited shout as he snorted whatever drug was on the table.

I waited against the wall, the Beretta pointed at the kitchen entryway.

Serafin's gun emerged, then his arm, his face, and his shoulders. I lowered the barrel of my gun so it was in line with his head.

He wasn't going to let us leave. None of them were, the murderers.

Psychos.

Druggies.

They weren't letting Dante and me go.

So I pulled the trigger, and Serafin's head split open.

I rushed over to the sofa and shot the other two before they could stand, then went into the kitchen, kicking the bottles and cans that were in my way, and took the roll of cash.

I didn't say anything to Dante as I passed. I didn't look at him or the gifts on the floor or the dead men. I just clutched the cash and left the house.

~

Dante was laughing, laughing and snickering the whole way back to the house on Durazno. "A beast!" He slapped me on the shoulder and took the roll of cash.

"So now what?" I asked when we'd gotten inside.

"What? You want more?" He shoved the money above a ceiling tile in the hallway.

"I mean the money. Do we get any?"

"That's for Javier to decide. You did kill three of his sicarios. That could be worth something. Or nothing. Depends on how he looks at it."

"They were going to kill us."

Dante nodded. "Possibly."

"They were. I didn't have a choice."

"Don't worry. I'll vouch for you. I've got your back." He took a breath, checked his phone, then said, "It's almost six. I'm going home."

"You don't live here?"

He laughed. "This is a *safe* house."

"Yeah? So?"

"You don't live in a safe house."

"Why not?"

"'Cause it never stays safe forever. Too much shit goes down here. Use it, and lose it. That's the rule."

"So we're going to stop coming here?"

"At some point." He hit me on the shoulder and headed for the door. "It's safe now, though. Stay and hang out if you want."

"No. If you're going, I'm going."

"Want a ride?"

"I've got my bike."

"Right." He turned around and looked up at me. "No offense, but you should get something a little cooler. A Lobo. Or at least a *real* bike."

I nodded, but my money was going elsewhere.

XI
The Boy

The sun, even at the end of the day, was brutally hot as I sped through the streets. The wind passing through the valley helped some, but it also meant the air was thick with dust, and by the time I got home, I was coated in a ghostly powder. A cold splash of water from the kitchen sink was going to be perfect, but as I pushed open the front door, that vision vanished.

"Jesus. What happened?" I cried.

I'd stepped into a mess worse than the sicarios' house. The couch had been flipped over, and the fabric sliced and torn open with chunks of white stuffing littering the floor around it. The drawings Isa and Katie had taped to the walls were ripped and scattered everywhere.

And the TV was gone.

And the frame with my dad's uniform and medal.

"What happened?" I called out.

"We're in here," my grandma said.

I jumped over the couch and bounced into the kitchen. My grandma and my sisters were wiping up the food that'd been tossed from the fridge.

"What happened?"

Isa and Katie both looked up at me. Isa had been crying, her face puffy and eyes red, but Katie had kept herself composed. At least until she saw me. Then she began to tear up.

"Are you okay?" I asked. "Are you hurt?"

My grandma got up from the floor, holding a rag dripping with milk. "Addicts. We leave for *one* minute, and those scum break in."

The radio was gone, and the shelf it'd been sitting on torn from the wall. The addicts just grabbed anything of value and trashed the rest.

"But you're okay?" I asked.

"We weren't here. We're fine."

"We needed tomatoes," Katie said. She glanced over at a paper bag on the counter under the window.

Isa pulled herself up from the floor and wrapped her arms around my waist. I hugged her back. "It'll be okay."

She pushed her head against my hip and mumbled something.

"What's that?"

Katie spoke for her: "She doesn't have any insulin."

Isa started to cry.

"Shit." I looked at my grandma.

She gestured at the vial on the table that was cracked and empty. "Scum."

"It's okay," I said. "We'll get you more." I gave Isa a squeeze. "I'll get you more."

She shook her head.

"We've got money. There's plenty in the envelope. I'll go get you some insulin right now." I unwrapped her arms from my waist and started for the bedroom.

"The envelope's not there," my grandma said.

"They took that too."

~

I kept pounding on Carlos's door. His car was out front, so he was home, but it took him forever to answer. When he finally did, my hand was throbbing.

"My house"—I pointed at it—"got robbed."

He titled his head to see around me. "I'll figure out who did it. Just give me a couple days."

"Isa's insulin," I said. "I need to get her insulin."

"Okay. Go get some. You got money."

"I don't. They found it."

Carlos just smiled and patted my shoulder. "You'll get more. El Paso's coming up."

"She needs her insulin *now*. She could die. DKA. She goes high and DKAs. Diabetics die from DKA."

"I have no clue what that means."

"Please, Carlos. Can I just borrow some money? I'll owe you."

"I don't like loaning people money."

"Javier," I shouted. "He'll give me some for today. Can you call him?"

"For today? The sicarios you shot?"

"Yeah. We got his money back."

Carlos shook his head. "I don't think you're getting anything for that. I was just talking to him. He didn't sound too happy."

"Shit." I stomped away from the house, turned back. "What do I do?"

Carlos thought for a moment. "How about let's just go see what they have at the hospital? They might give me something."

"Yeah. Great. Okay." I turned and raced to Carlos's Caprice.

"What kind of timetable are we talking about here?"

Carlos asked as he climbed into his car.

I waited until he'd leaned over and unlocked my door. "As soon as possible," I said.

He started the car and drive us toward the hospital. On the way, he said, "Javier wanted me to tell you that you better not do that in El Paso."

"Do what?"

"Kill anyone."

"But what if I have to?"

"You just can't do that there, okay?"

"I guess."

Carlos zipped the car around a corner, then suddenly sat up in his seat and leaned close to the windshield. "Is that BB?" He pointed at a little man in a gray hoodie walking past an abandoned convenience store. "Shit. It is. That's BB." Carlos yanked the steering wheel, jumped the curb, and stopped almost on top of the man. "BB," Carlos yelled as he burst out of the car.

The little man bolted, flying down the street.

Carlos circled the car, pounding on the hood, calling for me to get out and help.

BB was already halfway down the block, but I tore after him like Isa's insulin depended on it (which maybe it did), and I soon caught up. I reached out, grabbed the man's hoodie flapping behind him, and yanked him to the ground.

He squirmed and pushed and kicked, but I had him.

When Carlos came jogging over, I pulled BB to his feet and twisted the back of his hoodie around my hand so tight it made BB gag.

Carlos grinned wide and poked the guy in the chest. "Told you I'd get you."

"But I stopped." BB coughed and tried to spit but nothing came out.

"Is that right, you Oompa Loompa?"

"Honest. No more." He spat air again. "I'm not taking people to Paso anymore. It was a bad idea. My mistake."

"You still owe us," Carlos said.

"But"—BB shifted his weight from foot to foot—"but there's no money. I never got paid." BB rubbed a hand through his scraggly mane of hair. "Jonathan screwed me. He had my girlfriend murdered. You hear about that?"

"I heard you did get paid and you're holding out on everyone."

"No way. I got nothing. Honest."

"We're going for a ride."

"Oh, come on. Don't be like this."

I tightened my hold on the hoodie and marched BB to the Caprice.

Carlos looked at me. "We'll go to the hospital after we're done. This won't take long."

"Oh, come on," BB said again.

~

Carlos drove us to the Fronteriza barrio on the western edge of the city to one of the last streets before the desert and the mountains began. He pulled up to a small cinder block building in the middle of a trash-filled lot. The lower half of it had been painted a light blue, but the rest of it had been left bare and exposed, abandoned. The neighboring houses were gone, burned down, their cracked foundations the only things left to hint at their previous existence.

"Why're you doing this?" BB whined as I dragged him out of the car. "I can't pay you what I don't got." The little man went limp, trying to make things difficult, but I simply scooped him up and carried him to the house.

Carlos unlocked the door and swept his hand across a light switch, bringing to life a single bulb in the center of the room. A string of white holiday lights around the window flicked on a second later. Carlos pointed to a metal chair set directly under the bulb. "Put him there."

"I swear," BB went on. "I never got paid."

Carlos went to a closet and pulled out a roll of duct tape.

I dropped BB into the chair.

"I swear," he said.

"Nobody's buying that," Carlos said as he bound BB's ankles with the tape. "Especially Javier."

"I told that scumsucker," BB yelled, "and I'm telling you: Jonathan never gave me a cent."

I grabbed BB's shoulders to keep him still while Carlos taped his wrists.

"Please," BB whined.

Carlos tossed the tape into the closet, then took out his phone. As he sent a message, he said to BB, "Don't lie, dude."

"I'm not."

Carlos put the phone away. He dug through BB's pockets, pulling out a wad of cash, keys, a phone, a capped needle, and some coins. He pocketed the cash and dropped the rest to the floor.

"This isn't cool, you guys."

"You made your bed," Carlos said and walked across the room to the window with the holiday lights. He pushed aside the sheet hanging over it and scanned the street.

On the wall next to him was a painting of Santa Muerte, a bit like the one those druggie, baby shower killers had in their house. In this one, though, it showed her entire body. She wore a white gown and held a black globe in one hand and in the other, a scythe. I stepped over for a closer look.

"Dante put that up," Carlos said. "Wish I believed in that shit."

"Who's telling you I have money?" BB yelled.

"I don't believe in it either," I said. "Looks cool, though."

"They're lying," BB said. "Lying."

I pushed aside some of the curtain. It had suddenly gotten dark.

"Just be a couple minutes. Then we'll go," Carlos said.

I nodded, and we watched the street as BB went on with his pleas. After fifteen minutes of chatter, Carlos and I let the sheet fall back into place and turned to the man slumped in the chair.

"What?" BB asked.

Javier flung open the front door. "You elusive little fucker."

BB snapped upright. "I'm not holding out on you. I swear."

"Then why you hiding?" Javier stormed over to BB. "Huh? Why you hiding?"

"'Cause of Herrera."

"Herrera?" Javier circled BB, his boots clicking on the floor.

"Herrera."

Javier stopped and crossed his arms, swaying slightly from side to side. "I heard you the first time, you little puke."

"She got killed."

Javier made a fist and punched the palm of his other hand, smacking it in front of BB's face. "I should beat the living snot out of you, you know that?" He crouched to look into BB's eyes, their noses nearly touching. "Should I beat the living snot out of you?"

BB gave his head a tiny shake. "Please."

Javier grabbed him by the shoulders and shook him hard, jerking BB around, making his shaggy curls toss about. "I hate you little fucks," Javier yelled. "If you're going to take people north, then pay us our share. But to hold out on us? And then start trafficking kids?" Javier shoved BB, sending him and the chair tipping back on two legs. When the chair came back on all four legs again, he smacked his hands together, making BB flinch. "Fucker!" Javier yelled. He hopped away. "Why can't you just *listen*?" He turned and pointed at BB. "You work for me."

BB nodded.

"You don't ever, *ever*, do that shit again. You got that?"

"Yeah."

"What?"

"I got that."

"Bullshit." Javier lifted his shirt and pulled a gun.

"I got that," BB cried. "I work for you. I know. I know."

"No. You don't know," Javier yelled. He pressed the barrel of the gun between BB's eyes. "Get it through your head."

"It is!"

"It's *not*!"

"It is!"

"Fuck you." Javier pulled the trigger, and BB and the chair went tipping over. Javier wiped his face, looked at the back of his hand, then turned and left, saying, "Bury him before he bleeds all over."

I hadn't moved. I wasn't sure I should. I eyed Carlos, and Carlos eyed me.

When Javier's car started up outside, Carlos shrugged. "Don't mess with Javier," he said and went to the body.

We carried BB into the backyard, into the darkness just beyond where the light from the house could reach.

"Bring that over," Carlos pointed to a plastic industrial drum by the back steps. "We'll stick him in that, then bury him," he explained. "Keep the coyotes and shit away, you know?"

I rolled the barrel over and set it upright.

Carlos flicked the latches around the lid. "Can you lift him in if I hold it still?"

"Sure." I turned to BB. His back was arched slightly, because we'd dropped him on a rock, but that made for a good spot to grab him. I lifted, keeping my distance from his leaking head, and hoisted him up and into the barrel, dropping him in head first.

We had to bend and twist BB's legs to get him completely settled, but we made it work.

"Cool." Carlos put the lid back on. "Wait here a second." He disappeared into the house, returning a moment later with some shovels.

We dug for ten minutes, much faster than I had thought we could, spurred on by the occasional yip of a coyote just beyond the light.

When we rolled the barrel (and BB) into the hole, Carlos said, "Shit. Did I latch it?"

I shrugged. "Thought you did."

"Let's just say I did." He gazed around, breathing hard. "This whole place is a cemetery. Bodies buried fucking everywhere." He chuckled.

I looked out at the desert and shivered.

~

"Just wait here," Carlos said when we got to the hospital. "I'll see what I can get."

"Just take whatever they'll give you. Take all of it." I brushed a few more grains of sand from my arms.

He hopped out of the car.

"Tell them I'll pay them back," I yelled.

He flashed me a thumbs-up and vanished through the front entrance, but when he returned, he shook his head. "They're out."

"Out?"

"I can check some pharmacies tomorrow if you want."

"They're out?"

"Totally. A pharmacy will have some. I'll check first thing in the morning."

"But she could die. We have to get some now. I'll break in someplace. That pharmacy by the Superette. Drop me off there."

"The doc said to just have her drink water. Lots of water. She'll get through the night."

"Water?"

"He said it'll flush some of the glucose out of her system. Keep her from going too high."

"Isa's a brittle diabetic. That won't work."

"It's just one night," Carlos said.

I still didn't believe it, but I said, "I need to go home. Tell my mom."

Carlos nodded—"Yeah, okay"—and took us back to Joaquín Terrazas. He gave me a pat on the shoulder. "Come over tomorrow morning. We'll go get some insulin."

I managed a "thanks," brushed some more sand from my arms, and pulled myself from the car.

"Water?" I kept mumbling to myself as I crossed the street.

The flattened TV box was outside my house atop the pile of other random garbage-not-garbage things that we kept in case any of it proved useful later, and I realized that I'd caused this whole mess. It was the TV I'd bought. I'd ridden home with it cradled across my lap for all the world to see, including the addicts who'd broken in. I'd been so proud of my purchase.

"You dumbass," I hissed.

I stopped and looked down the street. I had to go to that pharmacy. I had to fix this. Now. I just needed something to smash a window or break a lock.

Where had I put that hammer I'd found in the mine? It was under the sink, wasn't it? Assuming the addicts hadn't taken it or tossed it somewhere.

I quickly snuck into the house and crept toward the

kitchen.

The place had been reassembled a little bit. The couch was back on its legs and the cushions, still torn open, returned to their places. Some of my sisters' artwork had even been tacked back on the walls.

Everyone was probably sleeping. The bedroom door was shut, but then my mom came rushing out of the kitchen. "Where were you?" she cried.

I jumped back. "I, uh, was trying to get Isa insulin."

"Who was that man? How do you know him?"

"Carlos?"

"Ingeniero."

"Ingeniero?"

"He brought us insulin."

My grandma came out of the kitchen. "Who's Ingeniero?" She got toe to toe with me, and looking straight up at my face, said again, "Who's Ingeniero?"

"Uh, I think that's Carlos's friend."

She glared at me, her lips pursed. "And why is Carlos's friend bringing us insulin?"

I looked at her, at my mom. I shrugged. "I don't know. To be nice?"

"He brought us three vials," my mom said.

My jaw dropped. "That's awesome."

"Who is this Ingeniero? What does he do?" my grandma asked. "Is he a narco?"

"I don't know what he does. I don't know him."

She pointed a finger in my face. "You don't talk to Carlos anymore. He's an Artistas Asesinos. Don't you talk to him."

"He's okay. He helps."

She stood on her tiptoes and smacked me on the forehead. "Are you stupid?"

I stepped back. "But we have Isa's insulin, don't we?"

"And now you've indebted us to them."

"You don't want the insulin?" I asked, raising my voice. "You want Isa to die?"

"How dare you," she shouted.

"I did a good thing. Isa has her insulin...because of me. Me."

My grandma pursed her lips, breathing long and deep through her nose. She sighed. "Because of you." She nodded her head, looked down at her feet, then around the room. "Yes, this has all happened, because of you." She quietly turned around and went into the kitchen, shaking her head.

My mom and I looked at each other. I said, "Isa's okay now," and she nodded.

XII

The Boy

The next day, Isa woke me up with a big hug. "Thank you, thank you, thank you," she said.

I pulled my arms out from under the blanket and hugged her back.

She gave an excited squeal. "There's *so* much insulin."

"I know. It's crazy," I said.

"Grandma's making breakfast. Pancakes. My tooth is loose." She stuck a finger against her upper incisor and gave it a wiggle.

"Cool. Is Grandma going to pull it out?"

"No," Isa groaned. "Gross." She rolled off the bed and ran out of the room.

I pushed the blankets away, threw on a gray T-shirt and jeans, then went to the kitchen after her.

Isa was clutching our grandma at the hip as she flipped pancakes at the stove. "Make mine *really* big," she said.

Katie looked up from the table. "Did you get me anything?" she asked, eyebrows arched.

"You want insulin too?"

She scrunched her nose. "If Isa gets something, why don't I?"

"What do you want?"

She didn't hesitate. "A tiara," she said with a smile.

Isa spun around. "I want a tiara too!"

"Two tiaras? I don't know," I said, feigning concern.

"Please? Can I have a white one?" Katie asked.

"I want red!" Isa shouted.

"Okay. Sure."

My grandma looked over her shoulder, scowling.

I didn't care. Katie and Isa were happy again, but it was enough to get me out of the house. She hadn't made enough pancakes for anyone other than Isa, Katie, and herself anyway, so I told her I was going to the roundabout to wash cars, and she waved her hand, shooing me away.

Of course, I didn't go to the roundabout. I went over to the house on Durazno. Dante was on the couch eating Pop-Tarts.

"You want one?" He held up the box, and I nodded, so he tossed me a pouch.

"Anything happening today?" I asked, biting into the frosted, strawberry pastry.

"Heading to Paso." He set the box aside. "Got your passport?"

"Passport?" I wiped the crumbs from my mouth. "I thought I didn't need a passport. You're not being serious, are you? Are you serious?"

Dante chuckled. "It's a joke."

"That's not funny. Freaking me out."

"You got your gun, though?"

I tapped my knuckle against the Beretta tucked under my shirt.

"We're meeting one of Javier's coyotes. We'll sneak over in his truck."

"Is it safe?"

"Does it matter?"

"I mean, I don't want to get caught." *I want my thousand dollars*, I was thinking.

"We won't get caught. We're taking the Puente Libre Bridge. It's busy. Especially in the morning. We'll slip right through."

"But if we got caught—"

"*If*," Dante stressed.

"—what would happen?"

"Nothing. Get turned around and sent back? I don't know."

"And then we try again?"

Dante took one, two, three bites, finishing his Pop-Tart, then got up from the couch. "Dude." He put his hands on my shoulders and gave a gentle shake. "You need to relax. Center your chi. It'll be fine."

I breathed deep and nodded.

"Good. Now let's go. Already wasted enough time waiting for your sleepy ass to show." He pulled out his phone and sent a message, then headed outside to the Lobo.

We ended up halfway across the city in the Hermanos Escobar Industrial Park. Dante stopped at an unmarked warehouse and pointed to a row of box trucks in the lot beside the building. "Just so you're clear," he said, "Javier wants this guy alive. No flipping him off any bridges."

"I'm not doing that again. Got a gun now."

"Dude, that's my point. Don't go crazy."

"Fine."

"You understand?" He glared at me.

"Yeah, I get it. Alive."

"This is important."

"I get it."

"Okay. Good. Then come on."

We climbed out of the Lobo and crossed through the lot, dodging semis and forklifts as they rumbled around. One of the box trucks was painted with brightly colored fruit, and Dante went up to the back of it. A round man in an orange t-shirt dropped from the cab and smiled.

"Tomas. How are you?" Dante asked, extending his hand.

"Could be better." Tomas shook Dante's hand, then mine. "Back aches. Neck hurts. Knees are going."

"Family good, though?"

"Nah. Wife left me."

"Shit. Really, man? That sucks."

Tomas rolled up the back door of his truck, saying, "I believe in two things: family and faith." A cool, sweet smell came out of the truck. "But my wife left me for my pastor, so I don't know what the hell's going on anymore." He looked at me. "Hop in."

I stepped up to the truck. Crates with stickers of little cartoon images of avocados, mangos, papayas, oranges, and grapefruit were stacked to the ceiling.

"Your pastor?" Dante said. "That's rough."

Tomas shrugged, then gave me a gentle slap on the arm. "Squeeze through all the way to the end there." He gestured at a gap between the left side of the truck and the crates. "Should be room enough to get through."

"Then what?"

"Then you knock on the back, and they'll let you in."

"Fucking pastors," Dante muttered to himself.

I grabbed the side of the truck, pulled myself up, and sidestepped into the space. My shirt kept getting snagged on the crates, pulling entire stacks to their tipping points, but I finally reached the back without getting crushed by the fruit.

I knocked, and a lock disengaged with a quick *shink*.

The wall, a hidden door, slid to the right, revealing a badly sunburned bald man. He nodded up at me before withdrawing into the space.

"There you go," Tomas said.

I took a half step in and glanced down the length of the compartment. There were six other people along with the sunburned man. Someone had a flashlight and swung it my way.

I stepped in, but I had to turn sideways to actually squeeze into the space.

"Right behind you," Dante said, easily popping in after me.

I shuffled next to the sunburned man as Dante slid the door shut. The man was holding a rosary, and he started pinching the beads between his fingers. Behind us, beyond all the crates of fruit, Tomas rolled the door down with a slam. The lock snapped into place.

"Make yourself comfortable," Dante said, settling beside me. "It's a long ride."

The truck tilted to the left as Tomas must've climbed into the cab.

"Lean back," Dante instructed. "And slouch down a little. Let your knees rest against the other side."

I did, but it kind of hurt, and I said so.

"Yeah, well, this is as comfortable as it gets," Dante said.

I took a breath of the sweet, cool, fruity air. "How long will this take?"

"Two or three hours."

"Huh? To cross the border?"

He nodded. "Just like cooking. Can't rush a good meal."

I slumped farther down, getting nicely wedged, so I wouldn't have to strain to keep my balance as the truck rumbled away.

After a few minutes, the truck stopped at what

seemed like an incredibly long traffic light. I even started to wonder if we hadn't pulled over, but then Dante said, "Morning on the Puente Libre Bridge. The slowest five hundred feet ever."

The sunburned man started over on his string of beads.

A voice suddenly boomed right outside our truck, "Water! Water here!," and I jumped.

"Relax," Dante said. "Just a vendor."

I took a deep breath. More voices came and went, calling out the prices of soda, snacks, and anything else a bored motorist might buy. "How many times you cross?" I asked Dante.

"A bunch. First time I was trying to run away. That one was freaky. And I *did* get caught then, but after that, when I started transporting mota and I knew the right people...easy."

"People like Tomas?"

"Yeah. He's the best. Why do you think he charges these guys"—he gestured at the sunburned man—"the big bucks?"

"Because he can?"

"Not if he's no good. But Tomas knows the border agents like you know your family. He knows who's just collecting a paycheck, who's at the end of his shift and ready to go home, who doesn't want to be tearing apart a truck right before the day ends."

The truck crept forward, moving a foot, idling for a minute, then moving another foot.

"And Tomas knows which guys want to be G.I. Joe. Never get in G.I. Joe's line."

The sunburned man went on shifting through his beads.

"Tomas knows them all."

I nodded and stared ahead at nothing as the vendors' voices faded and the truck jerked and stopped, jerked and stopped. After what felt like forever, the truck's engine shut off.

I stood up. "Did we run out of gas?"

Dante held out a hand. "This is normal."

A tapping, metal on metal, started up at the back of the truck and moved its way around us. Sweat dripped down my spine and caught in the waistband of my jeans. I squeezed my hands into fists and tried to take slow, deep breaths.

Then there was nothing but silence. The truck just sat there.

"I can't do this," the sunburned man grumbled.

"Quiet," Dante said.

"I gotta get out."

"Shut the fuck up," Dante hissed.

"I can't breathe." The man grasped his rosary and started to push me aside, trying to squeeze between me and the wall, but it was too narrow. "Move," he whined.

I grabbed him by the shoulders and tried to hold him still, but he kept wiggling and squirming.

"What the fuck, man?" Dante cried. "Chill."

I started to really squeeze down on the man, but then something heavy and metallic rumbled to life at the front of the truck, and we all froze, not realizing it was the engine until we began to move again.

The man laughed. "Oh, thank God."

"You dumb shit. You're fucking lucky."

The man settled beside me and kissed his rosary.

"Moron."

The truck picked up speed.

"Is that it?" I asked Dante.

"Just about."

The truck looped around an exit or something and got off the bridge. After a few more minutes of driving, when the air had really grown ripe and heavy with fruit and sweat and wood and metal and gas, the truck finally stopped for good.

Dante slid open the compartment door, and I followed him out, dropping from the truck into another lot filled with forklifts and trailers.

We had gone from one industrial park to another. I couldn't actually tell a huge difference between the two, except that the Franklin Mountains were now much larger than I'd ever seen them.

"You good?" Tomas asked us.

"Just peachy," Dante answered, pulling me aside so the sunburned man (who was grinning like an idiot) and the rest of the stowaways could climb out.

"Be right back, then," Tomas said before escorting the migrants to a building across the street. Tomas walked up to some guy who looked like he was on a smoke break. The man flicked his cigarette away, took an envelope from Tomas, then led the migrants inside. A moment later, a couple of guys in overalls came out, and Tomas pointed at his truck. The men nodded, Tomas said something that made them all laugh, then they parted.

When Tomas got back over to us, Dante asked, "When's he coming?"

"Should be any moment," Tomas said, drawing out the words, scanning the street. "Ah," he said. "Here we are."

A green minivan came whipping around the corner and pulled up next to us. Dante only had to reach out his hand to slide open the back door.

"What's up?" the man behind the wheel said.

"Hey, Hector." Dante gestured for me to climb in, so I did.

The man gave a nod in the rearview mirror. Hector was about as big around as Tomas, but he wasn't fat fat. Neither of them were. They were just beefy. They looked like bodyguards or bouncers, not couch potatoes.

Tomas took the front seat, and Dante got in beside me, sliding the door shut just before Hector sped off, driving out of the industrial park as fast as he came in.

"So what'd you find?" Dante asked.

"Jonathan's a busy guy," Tomas said, "but he keeps to a pretty regular routine. Thinks he's safe here, I suppose."

"Kind of is," Dante said.

"That *is* true."

"Where's he now?"

"The gym. This'll be the best spot to get him. He'll be tired after a workout. Won't fight much. And it's right off I-10 in a strip mall. Sunset Plaza."

"Where's he go after the gym?"

"He goes downtown, but we can't get him there."

"No?"

"His office is at 100 Stanton Tower." Tomas pointed at the skyline. "That brown one right there. It's across the street from the police station."

"Where's he go after that?"

"Home. But that's another tough spot. It's up in hills. Big fence. Security system."

"The gym, then," Dante said.

Tomas tapped Hector on the shoulder. "Told you."

"I never argued against it."

Tomas made a sound of dismissal, then went on telling us about what he knew of Jonathan from trailing him for the last several days. At that point, though, I wasn't paying much attention as I stared out the window and watched the city go by.

When we got north of the downtown, Hector turned off the highway and into the Sunset Plaza strip mall.

"Just to confirm," Tomas said, "we take him alive, but if he's trouble, we—"

"Don't let him be trouble," Dante interrupted.

"Well, right, but shit happens, so—"

"Don't let shit happen."

"But—"

"Tomas," Dante said. "Ingeniero wants Jonathan

alive. Full stop."

"Sure. Understood. When you get back with him, you make sure to tell Ingeniero that Hector and I appreciate what he's doing for us. We're very appreciative. You tell him that, okay?"

"He knows."

Tomas turned around to look at Dante. "Jonathan's got ninety percent of the market here; we're grateful to be getting that business. It's very generous."

"Ingeniero's a generous guy. Just don't start trafficking kids."

"Never."

I turned from the window. "Jonathan traffics kids?"

"He's a real saint, that guy," Tomas said.

As Hector found an open parking spot and backed into it, Dante said, "Ingeniero's got some sick torture planned out for this scumbag."

Tomas pointed to a Charger near the edge of the lot. "That's Jonathan's."

"And where's the gym?" Dante asked.

"Those tinted windows between Blockbuster and Whole Foods."

"The door with the peeling paint?"

"Yep."

"Looks like a dump."

"It's for show. It's members only. The inside is nice."

"Or so we've heard," Hector said. "We couldn't get in."

"Not unless we wanted to join for ten grand a year," Tomas added.

Hector leaned his head back against his seat. "Jonathan'll be out in ten or fifteen minutes."

It turned out to be twenty, but it went fast with Tomas talking about Jonathan and his trafficking of kids and how Hector and he would shut that down and run the city like honest people should. He was in midsentence, complaining about the Juárez Cartel and them trying to expand into El Paso, which he and Hector were fighting hard against, when a man in a tank top and slicked-back hair came out of the members-only gym. "There he is," Tomas chirped.

I sat up and reached for my gun but then remembered this wasn't supposed to be like that. "What do I do?" I hit Dante on the arm. "What do I do?"

"What do you mean?" he asked.

"I don't know what to do. What're we doing?"

"You grab him, for Christ's sake."

"Just grab him? But he's big. Look at his neck."

"You're big too," Dante hissed.

"He looks like a gorilla."

Tomas spun around in his seat. "I'll get him with this"—he held up a stun gun—"and you two grab him and shove him in the van."

Jonathan passed a tall woman in leggings and turned to watch her walk.

"Do we go now?" I reached for the door.

"Hold on," Dante said.

The woman vanished inside the gym, and Jonathan moved on.

"Now?"

"No. Just wait a second," Hector said. "I'm going to pull up to him."

Jonathan reached his Charger and popped the trunk. As he tossed his bag inside, Hector shifted into gear and raced from our spot.

"Go," Hector yelled as he stopped with a squeal behind Jonathan.

Tomas, Dante, and I threw open our doors and jumped from the van.

Jonathan barely looked at us before reaching into his trunk.

"No, you don't." Tomas lunged with the stun gun, and the cracking charge stiffened the trafficker's back.

But he somehow stayed on his feet, and grimacing, his teeth bared, he grabbed Tomas's outstretched arm and twisted, making Tomas cry out and drop the stun gun.

Dante went at the trafficker, but the gorilla man yanked Tomas around and threw him into Dante, sending them tripping over each other. I hesitated to do anything, and Jonathan gave me a quick shove in the chest, then took off running from the parking lot toward the road.

I pulled my gun.

"Don't," Dante called out.

I took a shooter's stance.

"Don't."

The trafficker's calves were huge. I wasn't going to miss. And then we could drag him back to the van and be gone. We could still get him, but just as I squeezed the trigger, Dante swatted my arms, and the shot went into the side of the van with a *ping*.

Jonathan galloped into the street, avoiding several skidding cars, and vanished into a ditch on the other side.

XIII
The Trafficker

I sprinted into the undeveloped plot of land across from the strip mall and dove behind a thick cluster of candlewood.

There was just the hum of traffic, kids yelling from inside a school gym, balls bouncing, and the wind whistling sharply through the spiny, dry plant.

I counted to twenty as the sun burned my back and the sand warmed my stomach.

When nothing changed, I edged around the side of the candlewood and took a look at Mesa Street (traffic was passing normally) and then the parking lot (the green van was gone).

I rolled onto my side and examined the spot where that fucker had hit me with the stun gun. There was a welt the size of my fist and as red as a cherry just below my ribs. It looked terrible, but it didn't really hurt. Maybe the workout and the adrenaline and the endorphins were counteracting the shock.

That's why I did those high-intensity workouts, after all. Put yourself through hell, and you can handle anything.

Probably surprised the shit out of those assholes.

I pulled my shirt back over the welt and got up.

The school bell rang, and the bouncing balls stopped. Traffic moved smoothly by. The world around me was carrying on as normal. No one had paid attention to what'd happened.

"Whatever."

I went back to the strip mall (waiting for traffic to clear before crossing Mesa Street this time) and returned to my Charger. The trunk was still open, but nothing was missing. Even the gun I'd been reaching for was still there, velcroed to the side. I slammed the trunk shut and got into the car, zipping over to my office in the Stanton Tower.

If those jackwads wanted to come at me again, then let them try. There was a police station across the street that offered plenty of protection, but the tower was also overflowing with its own security. (A bunch of shady criminal attorneys officed several floors down from me and demanded it.)

I swiped my keycard for the underground garage, waved at a security guy, then swiped it again at the elevator to get the doors to open, nodding to another security guy as he walked by. A camera in the upper corner of the elevator watched me as I rode up to the seventeenth floor, where I passed another security guy strolling down the hallway, taking in the Bob Ross-y artwork.

So yeah, good luck coming at me again.

I flicked on the TV for some ambient noise, then walked across the office and flopped into the chair I'd recently gotten as a gift from one of the maquiladora owners in Juárez. I couldn't remember exactly what I'd done for him, but it was supposed to be expensive. Ergonomic or whatever. It wasn't comfortable.

I grabbed the tennis ball sitting on the edge of the glass desk and threw it against the wall a couple of times, filling the small space with even more noise, but after a misthrow, the ball rolled into a corner, and that was the end of that.

I spun the chair around to the window and put my feet up on the divider between the glass panes, taking it easy for five or ten minutes (maybe even twenty), staring at the Franklin Mountains, before reaching over and grabbing the burner phone from my file cabinet.

When Alvaro answered, I said, "Ingeniero just tried to have me killed."

"Straight up?"

I dropped my feet and stood, putting a hand on the window, gazing down at the cars on the street. "He sent a couple of my competitors, Hector and Tomas. Plus a couple guys from down there. One of them had to be Ingeniero's new enforcer. Big lout."

"We'll go after Ing."

"You wouldn't even get close."

"Bet we could."

"If he had a family—"

"He doesn't."

"—you could *maybe* get his kid. Maybe."

"That's insulting."

"It's the reputation you're starting to create."

Alvaro asked, "What do you need?"

"See what you can find out about who those two guys were. Especially the big guy."

"And then kill him?"

"I don't know yet. Have to think about it."

Alvaro sighed.

"You don't have to kill everyone you come across. You'll get yourselves caught."

Alvaro laughed. "That's not likely."

"Just figure out what you can." I hung up and grabbed the tennis ball from the corner.

XIV

The Boy

"This crossing," Dante was saying as we stood in the back of Tomas's truck, "connects with I-10. And I-10 goes up and over to Dallas. It splits, and then from there, you can get to Oklahoma City, St. Louis, Atlanta, New York, Chicago, Minneapolis. Anywhere. Even go to Canada. All from this crossing here."

I wasn't really listening. I kept thinking of the thousand dollars I wasn't going to get, of the insulin Isa wasn't going to get.

"You know the percentage of drugs that crosses this bridge?" Dante went on. "Right at this *one* point. How much you think is passing through?"

I didn't answer.

"*Seventy* percent. It's crazy."

I actually hadn't said a word since Dante had knocked my shot wide.

"And they still—"

"Shut up."

"What?"

"We could've gotten so much money."

Dante was quiet for a moment, then he muttered, "Oh. Yeah, well, shit happens, don't it?"

"You let him get away."

"How do you figure that?"

"I was going to get him."

"Pfft. He was already gone."

"I had him."

"You're not *that* good of aim."

"I had him."

"And did you see there was a school across the way? Right where you were pointing?" Dante laughed. "You were freaking out about getting caught in this truck. You know what would've happened if you'd put a bullet in that school?"

"I wasn't going to miss."

"You were." Dante's phone buzzed, and after glancing at it, he said, "Javier wants us over at the shop."

"No. I'm going home. Just take me back to Durazno for my bike."

The truck was taking corners now, travelling down the city streets, getting close to the warehouse.

"No choice. Have to talk to Javier."

"Whatever. Such bullshit."

When the truck stopped and the back door lifted, I jumped out and went straight for the Lobo while Dante settled whatever payment was owed to Tomas. One of the warehouses across the street was marked up with a jumble of graffiti: a white skull, a black trident, a blue crown, and a mess of AAs over top it all, the mark of the Artistas Asesinos. The sight of this made me feel a little better. There'd have to be more opportunities to get some money.

But still, as Dante came over, I wanted to punch his face in. I shouldn't have to wait for another chance. I could've had my money today, and he fucked me over.

He saw me glaring at him and snickered. "Come on. Get in." He circled the truck and climbed into the cab, waving his hand at me like I was a child.

I punched the side of the truck, denting it, then got in.

"You need to chill," Dante said as he pulled out of the lot.

I slid down in the seat until my knees hit the glove compartment and said nothing.

We eventually stopped at a two-story building on Calle Murguía.

"What's this?" I asked.

The building stretched the entire block and housed a dozen small shops. Above us, billboards for Coca-Cola and Skwinkles candy leaned over the edge of the rooftop.

"Javier's office," Dante said and jumped out of the truck.

I flicked my seatbelt off and followed him down the sidewalk, both of us squeezing between tables and racks of crap that the shop owners had dragged outside. One had some plastic tiaras, their fake jewels sparkling under the sun.

Dante led me inside a tattoo shop on the corner. Some girl was getting a tattoo on her ankle while her friend watched, sitting across from her in a pool of sunlight coming through the windows. As Dante and I walked past, our shadows cast over them, and the tattoo artist paused for a moment. There were other tattoo stations, but there were no other customers, just one more tattoo artist by himself near the back, reading a newspaper.

Everything that wasn't a window or a mirror was covered with sketches of tattoos. Some were as small as a coin, others were large enough to cover a person's entire back. Dragons and crosses and guns, and in the middle of it all, Santa Muerte. She stared through a veil, her chin slightly lowered.

"That's cool," I said.

"Upstairs." Dante waved a hand, urging me to the back of the shop.

We climbed a worn staircase that groaned under my weight, and at the top, Dante stopped outside a closed door. He turned to me. "Just let him vent."

I shrugged.

"Seriously. Just let him vent." Dante waited until I finally nodded, then gave a quick knock on the door and went in.

Javier was on the other side of the room, sitting at a large wood desk, his feet up. Behind him, a crumpled map of Juárez was pinned to the wall. A knife had been stabbed into it somewhere in the downtown area.

Dante headed over to a leather couch in the middle of the room, and I followed him, trying not to trip over the cracked and uneven floorboards.

The space was as wide as the tattoo shop was deep with a row of dusty windows on the right looking out on an alley and the windows to the left watching the street. Some of the windows on both sides were open, and a hot, dry breeze passed through the room.

Javier stared at us, clenching and unclenching his jaw, making the muscles on the sides of his face bulge. He dropped his feet with a bang and leaned forward, resting his hands on the desk, letting them fidget around some lines of cocaine. He kept staring at us as his head dipped toward the white powder. He broke his gaze long enough to snort a line, then stood, twitching.

"So, maybe," he said, "I didn't tell you enough about what your job was with Jonathan. Maybe? Huh?"

Neither Dante nor I said anything.

"I don't know," Javier said. "Seems that way, because the key was that you"—he walked around the desk—"brought him the fuck back here."

I nodded in agreement.

Javier saw that and stepped a little closer, stopping next to a wooden pallet that had been propped up on cinder blocks in front of the couch. "We spent a fucking week making sure we could get him." Javier cupped his hand around his ear like he was holding a phone. "Bitch trafficker doesn't suspect a thing?" he asked. "Oh? He doesn't? Fantastic." Javier dropped his hand and scowled at us. "So I sent you over there to get the prick. You see?"

Javier was sweating and shaking, his eyes dilated, looking a bit like he had the other day when he'd killed BB.

"So how the fuck did the trafficker get away?" Javier yelled. He wiped some spittle from his lips. "Hmm?" He circled the pallet and poked me in the chest. "How? Niño?"

I side-eyed Dante, giving him a chance to explain what he'd done, but Javier wasn't willing to wait for an answer.

He went off pacing and muttering to himself, his face getting redder. "How? How? How?"

"I could've got him," I finally said. "But Dante stopped me."

Javier came at me, snarling. He clutched at his temples, shaking. "What?"

"Dante knocked my gun away."

"What?"

Dante shook his head. "The guy was already gone."

"Gone?" Javier grumbled. "So you, what? You let him run off?"

"We hit him with the stun gun, and he didn't go down. What else could we do?"

"You shoot the fucker," Javier yelled.

"Exactly," I said.

"In Paso?" Dante said. "No way."

"I told you to go get the guy. So you get him!"

"Come on, Javier. It's not that easy," Dante said, smirking.

Javier's eyes widened. Some weird animal sound

came from his throat, and he pulled a gun and pointed it at Dante. "You want me to show you how easy it is?"

Dante winced, but he didn't move away.

"Just send us back," I said.

Javier laughed. "I'm not sending you idiots back. I'm shooting you both in the head. Tiro de gracia. Easy!"

"We'll get him," I insisted.

"No," Javier yelled. "It's over, niño. A hundred thousand dollars, gone."

"A hundred thousand?" Dante said. "You didn't say it was that much."

"What's that fucking matter?" Javier pistol-whipped Dante across the face, sending him stumbling over the arm of the couch. "I *told* you to get him."

Dante didn't bother to try getting up. He just said, "Fine. We'll get him."

"You had your chance." Javier pulled the hammer back on the gun.

I pushed his hand toward the windows. "Don't. Just send us back. We'll get him."

Javier twisted his hand away and snarled, "You motherfuckers! You're taking sides against me?"

"No. No way," I said.

Javier looked up at me and snapped his teeth.

"I can—"

Javier shoved me.

I held my ground. "Javier. Stop."

He tried to shove me again, but I wasn't moving.

"Stop it."

He cried out and swung the butt of his gun, catching me across the chin hard, blurring my vision and making my knees wobble.

I tried to steady myself, but I just couldn't stay upright. I went down, and Javier was on top of me, howling and yelling and swinging, beating me, punching me, the gun and then his fist, one after the other.

I lifted my arms over my head, but he only got more enraged. He was going to step back and just start shooting. If I let him. So I reached out, wrapped my arms around him, pulled him close, getting cheek to cheek, and I squeezed him as tight as I could. His eyes bulged, and I snarled at him, "Stop it. Stop it."

The gun was pinned between us, the edges digging into Javier's chest as much as mine. He still had his hand on it. I felt his fingers wiggling.

"Stop it," I warned, squeezing harder.

The gun turned into me, digging into my breastbone. Javier's eyes narrowed. Maybe he was smiling.

So I turned my head and bit him, sinking my teeth into his nose, clenching as hard as I could, and then I pulled, tearing off skin and cartilage.

His eyes went so wide I could see more white than brown. I let go, and the noseless man dropped on his back, holding his hands to his face, a silent howl frozen across his mouth.

The room was utterly silent for a moment, then Javier inhaled deep and let it out in a long wail.

His chrome pistol lay between us on the floor.

I picked it up, stood over Javier, and put a bullet in his head.

~

"Holy fuck," Dante said.

I was sitting in the chair behind Javier's desk, the closest farthest thing from Javier that I could collapse into. I brushed away the cocaine.

"You killed him," Dante muttered from the couch. He'd uncurled from his fetal position, and was leaning over the arm, looking down at Javier.

I stared at the door, waiting for someone from the tattoo shop to come see what had happened, but either no one had heard or no one wanted to admit to what they had heard, so Dante and I were left alone.

"I had to," I said, setting the pistol on the desk. I only now noticed that it was a 9mm Beretta like mine. This one just had an etching of a skull spitting flames along the slide. I leaned over the desk, blood trickling down my face. Somehow I was feeling Javier's blows sharper now than before.

"You fucking bit his nose off." Dante turned from the body to me. "His nose."

I rested my chin on my arm and stared at him. My mouth was probably covered in Javier's blood. "I want to go get that trafficker," I said.

"Yeah. Anything. You got it."

"We can get him."

Dante nodded. "Yep."

"I want the money."

"It's yours."

I gestured with a nod at Javier. "What do we do with him? Bury him in the desert?"

"Maybe hang him from a bridge?"

"Javier?"

"If he just disappears, Aztecas will think we're vulnerable. One of them might even claim they did it. But if we hang him, we're sending a message: there's a new boss now."

"Who?"

Dante pointed. "You. The Beast."

I sighed. My head hurt so damn bad. I wanted to lie down, but I got up instead and searched Javier's pockets, finding a set of keys and two hundred dollars in twenties. I set the keys on the desk next to a cell phone and kept the cash (for Isa's insulin) before collapsing in the chair again. "Where you going to hang him?"

"The Benito Juárez Plaza would be good."

"Fine. Let's go."

Dante shook his head. "Not now. Carlos and I can do it." He then added, "It's a lot easier when they're already dead."

Someone from downstairs finally must've gotten the nerve to come see what'd happened, because the stairs started to squeak and whine.

"What do you want?" Dante called out.

The door opened, and Ingeniero stepped in, stopping midstride when he spotted the mess. He looked at Dante, then me. "What happened?"

I said, "He went all—"

"And what happened to his nose?" Ingeniero came in for a closer look.

"Mike Tyson," Dante said.

Ingeniero tilted his head to the ceiling, staring at the beams. "Lovely," he said with a long exhale.

"He went all crazy," I explained.

Ingeniero looked at Dante on the couch. "May I sit?"

Dante jumped off the couch. "All yours."

As Ingeniero snuck around the body and took a seat, he said, "Javier was a good captain. He listened."

"He went crazy," I repeated, then gestured at the welts on my arms. "And look at Dante's face. And"—I placed a few fingers on the top of my head, held them there for a moment, then pulled them away, showing Ingeniero the blood—"look."

He nodded. "And I'm guessing this is because of what happened in El Paso today?"

"We're going back," I said. "We'll get the trafficker."

"What happened exactly?"

Dante spoke up. "The guy's a horse. We stun gunned him, and he didn't go down."

Ingeniero turned to Dante. "There were four of you. One of which was him." Ingeniero gestured at me.

"I know, but Jonathan's some 'roid monster."

"So you'll go back? Try again?"

"Yeah. Absolutely," Dante said.

"Good." Ingeniero smiled. "You have a newborn, don't you?"

Dante scratched the back of his head. "Ah, yeah."

"You settle on a name?"

"A name?"

"The term by which you will address your son?"

"Oh. Going with, uh, Caro."

Ingeniero nodded. "That's a great name. Hopefully Caro has a chance to grow up to be a better listener than his father."

Dante gave a barely perceptible nod.

"It's good to have family to take care of." Ingeniero faced me. "Isn't that right?"

I nodded. "We'll get him."

"No. I will deal with Jonathan. Stay out of El Paso." Ingeniero lifted his hand when I started to say something. "You two just keep out of sight for a bit. Jonathan's a vindictive little freak. You both have targets on your backs now. Understand?" He waited until he'd received nods from us both, then looked down at Javier's body. "Anyway...Javier said he had some money for me. I was coming over to get it."

I pulled out the cash from my pocket.

"If that's all there is, we're in trouble."

Dante reached into his pocket. "How much are you looking for?"

"Ten percent of whatever you collected this month."

"Oh," Dante said. "A lot more."

Ingeniero nodded. "And that'll continue every month. My people, the police, the politicos, they don't come cheap. And the houses, the guns. It takes a lot to keep everyone safe. Give me my share, and I can keep your family safe"—he pointed at me—"and your Caro safe." He pointed at Dante.

"We'll find it," Dante said. "No problem."

Ingeniero stood up and took another look at Javier. "You better hang him."

"Tonight," Dante said.

Ingeniero stepped around the body and headed for the door. "Let me know when you find my money, please."

When he'd left and shut the door, Dante said, "If he tries anything with Caro, I swear to fucking God."

"What do you mean?" I asked.

"He's killed kids before."

"He wasn't saying that."

"Yeah, he was."

I studied Dante for a second and realized he was serious. "Can we go back to Durazno? I have to get my bike. I'm going home."

Dante went over to an open window and stuck his head out. After a moment, he popped back in. "Seeing if Ingeniero was still here. He's gone. Let's go."

We left Javier where he was and headed downstairs. The girl and her friend had left, and the tattoo artists were now both just sitting on chairs reading the paper. Dante pulled me over to a couple of sinks in the back, where we cleaned away the blood.

"For your chin," Dante said, handing me a bandage from the cabinet above the sink. He pulled out two more for himself and laid them across his cheek.

"This doesn't feel real," I said.

"The Band-Aid?"

"This. What's happened. All of it."

Dante slapped me on the shoulder. "You get used to it."

~

I got on my bike and went home. Isa was sitting at the end

of the kitchen table, and she turned and looked at me through the doorway, smiling, and I felt somewhat normal again.

I could hear the others in the kitchen, eating dinner. I knew I probably looked pretty bad, but I wanted to see them, so I went right in. "I'm okay. Don't worry."

"What happened?" My mom hurried around the table and inspected my face. "What happened?"

I gently pulled her hands away. "Just slipped climbing a fence."

"Your arms." She grabbed my hands and studied the red lumps.

I gave several nods. "Landed on some rocks. I'm fine." I turned to Isa and Katie. "Hey. I got something for you." I held up two little plastic bags. "For Isa"—I handed her a bag—"and Katie," I said, handing her the other.

The girls dug in and pulled out the tiaras I'd promised them, letting out little squeals of excitement.

"Look," Katie said, waving her white tiara at our grandma sitting beside her.

"Hmm," she said, not looking away from her plate for more than a second.

Isa set her tiara atop her head and smiled wide, displaying the gap where her incisor had been that morning.

"Your tooth's gone," I said.

She nodded, adjusted the tiara, and said, "Fell out at school."

My mom was still studying the marks on my face.

"I'm fine. Seriously." I turned away and helped myself to some of the baked chicken sitting on the stove. "When did it fall out, Isa?"

"During art. I swallowed it."

"Gross." I took my plate of chicken, passed by my mom still standing there, and sat at the table.

Katie asked Isa, "Did you go to the nurse's office?"

"I didn't tell anybody I swallowed it."

"Why not?" I asked, watching my mom finally take her seat.

"'Cause I don't want to leave art," Isa said. "That's my favorite."

"I like history," Katie said. "It's about Mexico. Like really long ago."

"When there were dinosaurs?" Isa asked.

"Aztecs," Katie said, her eyes getting big.

"I want to learn about Aztecs," Isa said.

"They shouldn't teach you that," my grandma interrupted. She looked at my mother. "Why are they teaching children about such a violent culture?"

"It's part of our history," my mom said.

"I remember learning about Emiliano Zapata," I said. "Not the Aztecs so much."

"Just as bad," my grandma said, shaking her head. "Why teach such things? Violence breeds violence." Her lips curled into a sneer. "It's out of control. Beyond fixing. We need to stay out of it." She stared at me.

"We can always go to El Paso," I said. "It's not hard to get across. Really."

She gave me a sad look. "It's *very* hard."

"Someday," my mom said. "We need to save our money."

"How much?" I asked.

"I don't know."

"It'll never happen," my grandma said. "Never."

I pulled the money I had taken from Javier's pocket and set it on the table. "Let's try."

Isa, Katie, and my mom looked at the pile, but my grandma didn't take her eyes off me.

"Your father hunted and killed boys like you," she said.

"And look what that got him," I said, immediately regretting the comment as she jerked her head back like she'd been slapped. "I'm sorry."

She snatched the bills from the table and shook them in my face. "What good does *this* do? This is nothing. You want to get us killed for *this*?"

I sat up. "So I should sell elote on the side of the road like grandpa, then? Get shot by the cartel anyway?"

"How dare you."

"At least I'm trying. And I'll make enough for us to leave. I *will*."

"You won't," she argued. "These people are savages."

"Then why'd Ingeniero bring us insulin? Why's Carlos always giving me jobs?"

"To manipulate you."

"Isa has insulin. And I'm getting money. Finally!" I pounded my hand on the table, making Katie jump.

Isa started to scrunch up her face, trying hard not to cry.

"I'm sorry. I'm sorry," I said again.

My grandma took a deep breath, exhaled, and said, "You should go."

"Go?" I turned to my mom, but her gaze was down in her hands now.

"Yes. Go."

"Fine." I got up and stormed out of the house.

XV

The Trafficker

By the next day, after having made some calls and talked to some people who weren't Alvaro and his brother, I'd learned Ingeniero's new enforcer was a boy (a boy who'd eaten more than his fair share of Wheaties, but still just a boy).

I walked onto the balcony thinking about this, shaking my head at the corruption of today's youth. I set my coffee on the railing and stared down the side of the mountain. I probably shouldn't have been surprised by this. Ingeniero loved working with the impressionable. And with Mexico giving kids under the age of fourteen legal immunity to do whatever the fuck they wanted, why wouldn't the cartel recruit them?

Maybe if I'd been given such a free pass, I would've done a little more earlier on instead of waiting until I'd been a senior in high school. I had had some pretty messed-up thoughts as a kid. Who knows? I might've become some tiny John Dillinger and blasted away.

I kicked the lounge chair so it faced Mexico and took a seat. This early in the morning, the balcony was still in the shade, and with a soft breeze coming up the mountainside, I just tried to relax. I took my coffee from the railing, sat back, and sighed, still trying to get myself settled after yesterday's events.

I hadn't returned home until around midnight, having hunkered down at the office until I was relatively sure that the sicarios were gone. But even after emerging from the garage, it'd still taken me another hour of meandering through the streets of El Paso before I got truly comfortable that no one was coming after me, and I could head home to Thunderbird Drive, where I had a gun in every room, a tall concrete perimeter wall, and a security system that went off when even the smallest of birds landed nearby. This was all probably overkill, since I lived in El Paso and not Juárez, worlds apart even though only separated by a narrow concrete river, but I still needed to maintain my sanity. After all, the border obviously didn't protect me a hundred percent.

I sipped my coffee, studying the valley, my mind on that boy, Ingeniero's new enforcer. Maybe he didn't even understand the consequences of his choices, youth being so blind to foresight. He surely had to have experienced death in its various forms by now, but did he appreciate it?

Unlikely.

If I could have, I would've just given him a warning, but it wouldn't have gotten through. Not at his age. I had to do something drastic.

And then maybe Ingeniero and I could have a civil discussion. He just had to live with the fact that I knew what he was doing down there and trust that I didn't care.

XVI

The Boy

I ended up spending the night at the tattoo shop, lying on the couch in the upstairs office. At one point, Dante and Carlos showed up and took Javier's body, but the rest of the time I spent by myself, just looking at the beams running across the ceiling, thinking about family. I fell into some form of feeble sleep a couple of times, but it didn't last. When the sun started to rise, the phone Carlos had given me so long ago (or so it felt) rang.

"Daniel Salas is in Juárez," Carlos said after I'd answered. "We need to help run security."

"What's that mean? Who's Salas?"

"A boss from Sinaloa. Where are you?"

"The tattoo shop."

"Stay there. I'll be right over." Carlos hung up.

I got off the couch and stared at the floor where Javier had died. I'd wiped up most of the blood with some rags from downstairs, but a lot of it had already soaked deep into the wood, and had left a dark stain that kind of looked like a devilish grin. The more I stared at it, the more it freaked me out, so I grabbed my shoes and got out of there.

While I waited for Carlos down on Calle Murguía, I wandered through some of the shops. I was thinking about buying my sisters some fairy wands (the kind with star-shaped ends filled with glitter) to go with their tiaras when Carlos pulled up in the Lobo. "Maybe later," I told the shopkeeper.

Carlos pointed to the back after I'd climbed in. "That's April and Ashley."

I turned around and recognized the faces looking back at me. "Hello," I mumbled to the girl who'd been getting the tattoo. She was prettier than I'd realized, both her and her friend.

"I'm Ashley," she said. "She's April."

I smiled and repeated the hello. "What're those for?" I was looking at the four assault rifles (AR-15s) that rested between them.

Carlos said, "Security detail."

Ashley lifted one up and handed it to me.

"You know how to use that?" April asked.

"My dad let me shoot one when I was little."

"How little?" Ashley asked.

"Little enough it knocked me on my ass."

The girls shared a laugh, and I could feel my face redden. I turned to the front and pretended to be busy checking the ammo and the cleanliness of the chamber, while Carlos took us across the city.

"Where're we going?" I eventually asked.

"Almost there," Carlos said.

We passed a few police cars outside the airport, and I lowered the gun. "We're not going in there, are we?"

Carlos turned onto the entrance road. "Sure are."

"But why?"

"Told you. Security detail."

Outside the terminal, there were five black trucks waiting single file at the curb, and Carlos pulled up behind the last one.

I asked, "What do I do?"

"Hang tight. Keep an eye out for trouble," Carlos said.

"Shoot anything that moves," Ashley added.

Carlos laughed. "No, don't do that. Christ, Ashley. He'll believe you."

"That's why it's funny."

April tapped me on the shoulder. "No. Only shoot if you *absolutely* have to. We're low on ammo. Please don't waste it."

The phone in the center console buzzed, and Carlos read the message. "Ingeniero says Salas is in the middle truck."

"The middle truck?" Ashley asked. "The Lobo that's two ahead of us?"

Carlos said, "That one or the Suburban ahead of it."

"Okay, well, that's not really helpful."

The truck at the front of the line started to move, and we all followed.

I pulled the AR-15 to my chest, finger near the trigger. Our convoy of black, window-tinted vehicles cruised from the airport and onto Highway 45, speeding north, cutting through the heart of Juárez. We didn't stop at any of the traffic lights, just sped right through, sometimes cutting into the opposite lanes to bypass the cars waiting at the light. I held my breath each time we rushed into an intersection, but at the sixth set of lights, I finally saw that there were police cars blocking the cross traffic for us. Once we passed, they went racing ahead to the next set of lights. This went on for miles, and I couldn't help but grin, feeling a bit like I was the president.

We eventually took a right onto Manuel Gomez Morin Boulevard, then the vehicle I'd decided Salas was in, the Lobo, made an abrupt left turn down a side street, abandoning the rest of us.

"Where's he going?" I asked, turning around in my seat, watching the Lobo vanish.

"Don't know," Carlos said and continued down the boulevard. "Always happens. Don't worry about it."

He pulled a U-turn at the next intersection and headed back west toward our barrio. "Good job, team."

XVII
The Sicario

"B's really missing, isn't he?" Nemesio said. We were driving through the streets of northwest Juárez, passing squat homes shoved tight against one another.

"We should just forget about him," I said, glancing down a narrow pathway between houses. There were a few cars parked on it, barely squeezed in. Only motorcycles could pass through now.

Nemesio slowed down, so we could look around, then continued on.

I tugged at my shirt, pulling it from the sweat developing across my chest. We had rented a car, a sad, old Chevy Citation, so we wouldn't draw attention to ourselves cruising through Angeles, La Paz, Insurgentes, Cardenas, and Mesita. We thought we'd been clever getting a junker, but it didn't have working A/C, and we were getting cooked.

"You want to forget it?" I asked.

"There's Naranja," Nemesio said, pointing at our fruit-vendor friend up the road.

"After him, let's go. Take this piece of shit back."

"Just roll your window down some more."

"It doesn't go any lower. It's stuck." I yanked on the lever. "See?"

Nemesio parked the Citation and got out. I flung open my door but stayed in the car to avoid the only thing worse than no A/C, which was standing directly under the sun.

"Hey," Naranja chirped. "How you guys doing?"

"Need some intel." Nemesio looked over the fruit on display.

"What kind of intel?" Naranja pointed at an apple, and Nemesio picked it up.

"Looking for BB. You seen him?"

"BB? He got in some trouble."

"Yeah, with us." Nemesio turned the apple over a couple of times, then put it back.

"No." Naranja chose another apple and handed it to my brother. "With some guys from Cardenas."

Nemesio gave Naranja a couple of coins, then bit into the apple. "So the Cardenas guys, they kill him?"

"Maybe."

"Maybe?"

"I'm pretty sure."

Nemesio turned to me, swallowed. "Guess that's our answer, then."

I shrugged. "Hey, Naranja. You know anything about Ing's new enforcer? Supposed to be some big kid."

"How big?"

"Giant."

His brow furrowed. "Carlos was with a pretty big kid last week. Hadn't seen him before."

"Carlos who?"

"Villarreal. He's over on Joaquín Terrazas. Joaquín

and Calle Higuera."

"You don't know the kid, though?"

Naranja shook his head. "I can ask around."

"You do that." Nemesio gave Naranja several more bills for the information, then returned to the Citation. "So that's it for BB, huh?"

"That's it." I reluctantly pulled my door shut.

"Go see what the story is with Carlos and this kid?"

"Think we have to."

Our network covered the city like a web, so we just kept driving around, basically taking up the entire afternoon talking to shopkeepers, waiters, cabbies, couriers, barbers, and anyone else that wanted a small handout from Hermanos de la Muerte.

Carlos turned out to be some low-level AA not worth our time, but the kid was something else. People called him The Beast, and The Beast, people said, had just killed his own barrio captain. He'd apparently torn off the guy's face, then hanged the mutilated body upside down from the pedestrian bridge near the stadium.

"The Beast," Nemesio muttered as we left another halcon, some snotty little kid on a bike who thought he was going to be a narco but would probably just get himself killed in some crossfire. "Sounds like a maniac."

"Ing's playing with fire."

I eyed a couple of skinny, half-dead dealers standing on the outskirts of a dried-out park.

"Like Tyson and his tigers. Ing's going to get so fucked up."

"Should make Jonathan happy. You want to go check out Joaquín Terrazas?" I asked. "See what's there?"

He nodded and turned us around.

"Take Ordaz," I said, pointing at the turnoff for the viaduct. "It's a good shortcut."

"When it's not flooded."

"Does it look flooded?"

"Whatever."

We dipped into the viaduct, and Nemesio gunned it. As we passed under several low bridges that carried the street traffic across, I asked, "Wasn't a guy hanged from one of these last week? Some cop?"

"Something like that."

"Think The Beast was behind it?"

"Probably."

When we got to the street Naranja had given us (and confirmed by a few others), Nemesio pulled over at the corner. It looked like any other street. Piles of sand everywhere, garbage blowing around, dozens of wires overhead. I snapped a few pictures with my disposable Kodak as we watched and waited. Eventually, we got what we needed and left to get something to eat.

XVIII
The Boy

With Ingeniero warning me about the trafficker holding grudges, my head was on a swivel as I rode over to meet Carlos. And instead of whipping around the corner onto Durazno like normal, I took it nice and slow, creeping almost, which gave me time to pull to the curb when I saw a new SUV parked outside the house, its engine running.

I reached for my gun (Javier's chrome Beretta) tucked against my hip, but then stopped and went for my phone under the seat to call Carlos.

The doors on the SUV opened. I froze. Three figures in black hopped out.

"Shit." I yanked the gun from my waistband.

The figures stepped toward the house, lifted their assault rifles, and fired.

I jumped off the bike and took a shooter's stance, but I didn't pull the trigger. What was my Beretta going to do as the house popped and chipped and exploded with holes? I'd get mowed down just as fast.

When the gunmen finally stopped and had jumped back into the SUV, vanishing around the corner, I slipped the Beretta back into my waistband.

Our Lobo then came around the back of the destroyed house, the engine revving hard and its tires sliding in the sand. It raced onto the street and turned toward me. As it passed, Carlos waved from behind the wheel, so I jumped on my bike and followed him all the way to the tattoo shop.

"Are you okay?" I asked as he dropped out of the truck and smiled.

"Yeah. Totally fine. That was a rush, huh?"

"Was that the trafficker?"

"Jonathan?" Carlos shrugged. "Nah. Those were Aztecas. Had to be."

"Because Javier's gone?"

"That's what I'm thinking." Carlos slipped between the vendor tables, and went into the shop, nodding to the tattoo artists at their stations before heading up to the office. "They're testing us." He crossed the office, the floorboards creaking underfoot, and flopped down on the couch.

"What should we do?"

"Have to hit them back." He clapped his hands together. "Fast."

I stepped over to a dusty window, wiped it clean, and glanced out. The wind had whipped up the sand out in the desert and carried it over the city. The sun was now fighting to pass through the haze. "What does that mean, 'hit them back'?"

~

It meant we went out that night and shot up one of their houses. Which then meant the following night, the Aztecas went out and hit some house in our barrio, forcing us to hit another one of their houses the next day, and then they did the same the day after.

It meant that Carlos, Dante, and I had to get together and figure out how to really hurt them, because this wasn't going to stop.

"We need more intel," Dante was telling Carlos. "Someone must know something."

"I'm working my people," Carlos said. He was sprawled out on the couch, staring at the ceiling.

"We can't just hit another random house. We have to *hurt* them."

I groaned and leaned back in the desk chair. "Why'd I do that to Javier?"

"Because he was going to kill us," Dante chuckled from his spot behind the couch.

I waved at the air, at nothing, at everything.

"This is normal," Carlos said, pulling himself off the couch. He went to a window and scanned the area. "We just don't have the firepower we used to."

I sat up and started digging through the desk drawers. Javier had a thin black notebook in one full of names categorized under headlines like Bars, Clubs, Restaurants, Businessmen, Doctors, Lawyers, Border Agents, Cops. "Who are these people?"

Dante craned his neck, trying to see what I had in my hands.

I lifted the notebook.

"Oh. Those are our friends."

I pointed at the page titled Cops. "A lot of the names are crossed off. They're not friends anymore?"

"They're dead."

"That's a lot."

"Cops don't last long," Carlos said. He pulled his phone from his pocket and read a message. "We need to run security for Salas. He's leaving. Heading back to the airport."

"Now?" I asked. "I don't want to go out. Not now. Not with everything going on."

"That's why he's leaving," Carlos said.

"Don't blame him. I'd leave too," Dante said.

"I wouldn't," I said.

He smiled. "Good for you.'

"Salas is a coward."

Carlos turned to the door. "It'd get worse if he stayed and something happened to him. Salas is like Javier times a hundred."

"Times a million," Dante said, walking out with Carlos, leaving me to catch up.

Out on the street, April and Ashley were waiting in a black GMC Suburban. Dante and Carlos climbed into the back next to April, so I got into the front. Ashley gave me a stiff smile, then pulled into traffic.

"We have those AR-15s again?" I asked.

"Oh, uh, yep." April pulled the rifles from a bag in the back and handed them out.

"Shoot anything that moves, right?" I joked as I took one from her.

"What?" Her face was emotionless.

"You told me last time to shoot anything that moves."

"Oh. Ha ha. Yeah, Ashley said that." April sat back in her seat and turned to the window.

I looked at Ashley, and she was staring ahead, pretending to focus on the traffic. "Something up?" I asked.

"I think they're nervous around you," Carlos said. "Must've just heard about what you did to Javier."

"We're not nervous," Ashley said. "Just kind of...you know...I don't know."

April asked, "It's true? You bit his nose off?"

"The Beast," Dante roared as he clicked something in place on his rifle. "Welcome to the jungle." He began to hum the Guns N' Roses song.

"It is what it is," Carlos said.

I started to explain what had happened, but Carlos slapped me on the shoulder.

"It is what it is," he repeated. "Right?"

I nodded and kept quiet, leaving Dante to go on humming until we'd gotten all the way to about the spot where Salas had abandoned the convoy before. "You know where you're going?" he asked.

"I wouldn't be the one driving if I didn't, genius." Ashley leaned over the steering wheel, glancing at the houses around us, some hidden behind walls of shrubs, others unprotected, just set back from the street on lush green yards. "There." She pointed up the road, "2428 Calle Senecú."

Carlos peeked over her shoulder. "Fancy."

He was talking about the security wall, not the house, because all we could see were the tops of bushes and trees behind a glossy white wall decorated with wood carvings (and barbed wire).

Ashley pulled up to the front gate and rolled down her window, announcing our arrival to the intercom poking out of a small palm cluster. A second later, the gate swung open and revealed an ornate brick driveway.

"*Very* fancy," Carlos said.

The driveway took us beneath a canopy of palm trees and to a courtyard with a giant water fountain in its center.

"So fancy," Carlos said.

"Shut up," Ashley groaned, pulling to a stop near the fountain, behind three more black Suburbans.

"Why is Salas leaving this place?" I asked. I'd never seen a bigger house in my life. It looked like a hotel with its massive front doors and rows of arched windows. There were four garage doors way at the end, and guards were positioned outside them all.

"Shows you how bad he thinks it's getting," Dante

said.

"I'll watch the place for him while he's gone," Carlos said.

"No shit you would. We all would."

"Let's sneak back when he's gone," April said.

"And get a bullet in the head from a guard?" Dante huffed. "No thanks."

Another truck pulled up behind us, which must have been all we were waiting for, because after that, a guard by the front doors waved his arm for everyone to get moving. The convoy went curling around the fountain.

As we passed the front doors, though, the guard held up his hand and stepped in front of our Suburban.

"And what are we waiting for, buddy?" Ashley asked while the three Suburbans in front of us continued down the driveway toward the street.

"Salas," Carlos said as a garage door lifted and a Lobo rolled out.

The guard stepped aside, and we continued on, rumbling down the brick driveway and out into the street, picking up speed.

The convoy turned a corner, then another, heading toward the main boulevard. The path was clear except for someone coming down the other side of the street. I was watching them, this Ford Lobo, thinking, "Shoot anything that moves," and maybe I should have, because the Lobo veered, jumped the tree-lined median, and skidded to a stop in our path, bringing the convoy to a halt.

Something to our right let off a piercing shriek, and a wisp of smoke went streaking by our windshield, hitting the first vehicle in the convoy. The SUV exploded in a fireball, lifted into the air and tipped on its side, burning.

Another shriek and another bit of smoke, and the pavement next to Salas's Lobo erupted, tearing open one of his tires with a deafening boom.

I yelled, "Aztecas," and jumped from the SUV.

"You crazy?" Carlos or Dante yelled.

Bits of pavement were still raining down, pinging off the top of the vehicles, as I lifted my rifle and aimed at the bushes from where the rockets had come.

The guy tried to run. He sprinted from his hiding spot and headed around a house, but I cut him down. Three bullets in the back.

I turned to the Lobo that was blocking our way and fired off a couple shots, spiderwebbing the windshield, but I heard a motorcycle coming up behind me and spun around.

The rider, some fat asshole with stringy, long hair, lifted his gun.

I tapped the trigger of my weapon first—one, two, three times—and the rider jerked back. His gun bounced across the pavement as the bike continued on with the dead man atop it. The front wheel wobbled, and the bike collapsed, sending up a tail of sparks and dust as it skidded to the curb.

I jerked back around, and without taking my eyes off the Lobo down the street, raced to Salas's vehicle.

The heat from the burning tire was wild, but I knew what I had to do. I reached through the cloud of thick, black smoke engulfing the truck and yanked on the back door. It was stuck. I jumped back and screamed at Salas. "Kick it open."

There was movement down the street. Two men were jumping out of the Lobo. I fired, but my eyes were burning and watery. I couldn't aim. I just let off a round of bullets. The Aztecas scurried behind their truck.

I threw myself back at Salas' Lobo, into the smoke, and tugged on the door. It finally popped open as a bullet from the Aztecas pinged against it.

"Come on. Hurry." I reached into the smoke-filled backseat, felt a shoulder, felt a chest, grabbed a fistful of suit jacket, and pulled Salas out.

As I got the man on his feet, the Suburban in front

of us was reversing hard. Bullets from down the street were pecking at it. I shot twice at the Aztecas.

The Suburban stopped beside us, and the back door opened.

Salas gave me a quick pat on the arm, then disappeared into the SUV, which sped off, hopping the curb, kicking up dirt and grass, and racing away between the houses.

I turned back to the Lobo, catching one of the Aztecas as he tried to jump into the truck to give chase. The other man remained hidden until a couple of police cars, our escorts, came rushing down from the boulevard. When he tried to run, I shot him too.

~

"Are you fucking crazy?" Dante yelled after I'd climbed into the Suburban.

"What?" I buckled my seat belt. "Salas needed help."

"You don't run into shit like that."

"Shoot anything that moves," I said. "It worked." I smiled at Ashley, but she didn't smile back.

"Get us out of here," Carlos told her.

As Ashley took off, the SUV got quiet.

"I had to do *something*," I finally said.

"That could've been the army," Dante said. "They had rockets. You don't fuck with the army."

"It wasn't, though."

"If that was the army, man."

"It *wasn't* the army."

"Do you *not* get it, you stupid asshole?"

"Hey," Carlos said. "He saved us. He went out there, put his life on the line, and saved us."

Ashley ran a red light.

"Saved us, my ass. They had fucking rockets,"

Dante yelled. "Who runs into *that*?"

"Me," I said, looking at the AR-15 in my hands.

Dante didn't say anything, he just breathed through his nose, quick and heavy.

"Circle around some, Ashley," Carlos said. "Make sure we're not being tailed."

I held up the rifle for everyone to see. "Can I keep this?"

"Absolutely not," April said.

I turned around and looked at Carlos. "I think I need one, though."

"You need your head checked, that's what you need," Dante said.

I ignored him. "Can I get one?"

"Maybe we can see what The Gunman has," Carlos said.

"If you're ordering from The Gunman, get us some ammo," Ashley said.

"I could use a new 9mm," April said.

"Can we get rockets too?" My voice rose more than I intended.

Dante snickered. "Rockets? How about one of everything?"

"Everything?

"Just shut up. You're not getting rockets. We've got no money."

"You said you found Javier's money. How much was that?"

"You found it?" April asked. "Where?"

Carlos said, "Behind the map in the office. Two hundred thousand."

"What?" I gasped. My insulin problems were over with that much money.

"It's barely anything," Dante said.

Ashley pointed at the rearview mirror. "We're good. No tail."

"Take us back to the shop," Carlos said.

"Sounds like plenty to me,' April said. "Let's get at least a few guns and ammo. Spend a little money. Javier was such a freakin' tightwad."

"He wasn't a tightwad," Carlos said.

"What was he doing with it, then? Hookers in El Paso?"

"That was once."

"More than once."

"It goes to bribes and shit."

"Screw the bribes. We *need* guns," April said. "Buy us some guns. Look at what the Aztecas are doing. What happens the next time?"

Carlos was quiet for a moment, then said, "Dante, you want to go see what The Gunman can get us for ten grand?"

"Fifty grand," April said.

"The bribes. We can't *not* pay anyone this month. They'll dump us."

"You'd rather the Aztecas just kill us?"

"We'll be okay with ten," Carlos said.

~

Dante and I were in the Lobo heading south on the Periférica Camino Real Highway. He said he was bringing me along because, "The Gunman's a weirdo."

"What's that mean?" I asked.

He didn't bother explaining.

"You still pissed about what I did for Salas?"

He just kept driving, chewing his lip.

"You are. I had—"

"Screw that," he mumbled and veered off at the next exit.

"What're you doing? We need guns."

"Checkpoint. By the Cristo statue."

I looked back at the highway. There was a military truck with a machine gun mounted to its bed parked sideways across the road. "So?"

"Fuck that," Dante said.

"Okay."

"They're the problem, you know? Them. Not us. We can police ourselves. They just cause trouble."

"That's not true."

"They took my uncle once. He hadn't done a damn thing, but they held him in some military bunker for a month. Tortured him. Beat him. Starved him. For doing nothing. Not a damn thing. They're the reason people go north. Fucking military. It's got nothing to do with the cartels."

He was quiet for a moment, maybe waiting to see what I thought of what he'd just said, but I couldn't think of anything more than, "Hmm."

He went on. "You hear about them shooting Miss Sinaloa? Chased her down with a helicopter...When she got out of her truck, they shot her...With one of those huge-ass chopper guns...Some little beauty pageant lady. Christ. They do that shit every day. What kind of psychos are they?"

"My dad wasn't psycho," I grumbled.

"*Who* wasn't psycho?"

I changed the subject. "You want to get some food later?"

Dante shook his head. "I'm laying low after this. If there's military assholes out, shit's *really* getting bad." He turned from the side streets and rejoined the highway south of the checkpoint.

"That's why we need rockets," I said.

This time, he just went, "Hmm."

We drove for another mile before stopping at an ochre-colored home surrounded by a thick cement wall and metal gate. It wasn't the grandeur we'd seen over at Salas's place, but it was nicer than ninety-nine percent of the other homes in the city.

"Pays to be the guy who supplies the weapons," Dante said as he took out his phone and sent a message.

The gate slid open.

"Let's go." Dante jumped out of the truck.

The Gunman was waiting on his front steps in dark jeans and a flannel vest over a button-down shirt. He grinned but kept his head down as we walked up. Dark round glasses matched the black curls of his hair. "Hello. Please come in. Enter, enter." He held the door open with one hand. In the other, he was squeezing the handle of a fillet knife.

Dante nudged me inside.

"Let's sit out on the patio," The Gunman said after he'd shut the door behind us. "Nice day."

"It's kind of hot," Dante said, but the man was already heading down the hall to the back of the house. "Whatever." Dante pushed me ahead, then trailed after.

The house was clean and white. The floor tile, the walls, the doors. Even the pictures and diplomas spaced in even intervals down the hall were framed in white and centered on white cardboard.

Outside, the purity of it all continued with a white L-shaped wicker sectional, crushed white stone, and yucca plants potted in white planters. The Gunman took a seat, resting the knife on the cushion next to him. Dante and I went to the other end, not just for the shade of the palm trees.

The Gunman watched a couple of sparrows flit around above us, then he glanced down at the stone around his feet. "It is a little hot. I should get you something to drink. Water?"

Before we could answer, The Gunman picked up his knife and hurried inside.

"Don't drink the water," Dante warned me.

I nodded. "Okay."

While we waited, I asked, "You see all those diplomas in the hallway?"

"He used to be an econ professor or something."

"Where?"

"Mexico City. He worked on NAFTA."

"And now he's doing this?"

"Yep."

I gazed around the patio. There was some kind of sandy square patch off in the back corner with a few large stones. The sand was raked around them in even, circular patterns.

The curly-haired man returned with the glasses of water balanced in one hand and the knife held tight in the other. He gave us the waters, then sat. "So, business," he said, placing the knife back on the cushion beside him.

"Need some guns," Dante said, not touching his water.

"'Guns.' That's vague." The Gunman turned his attention to the crushed stone around his feet.

"Two AK-47s and six AR-15s," Dante clarified.

"And ammo," I added.

"How much ammo?" The Gunman asked.

I looked at Dante, and he said, "Three thousand rounds."

The Gunman's hand crept over to the knife's handle, and he started tapping a finger in slow rhythm. "Okay," he finally said. "Seventeen hundred for each AK-47. Twelve hundred for each AR-15. One thousand three hundred twenty for three thousand rounds of .223-caliber ammunition. That's eleven thousand nine hundred twenty."

"Can you make it ten grand even?" Dante asked. He set the water glass by his feet.

The Gunman shook his head. "No deals." He repeated his number. "Or," he said, "take away one AK-47 and 500 rounds of ammunition. That's an even ten thousand."

"How do you know that?" I asked.

"It's just math."

"Fine. Whatever," Dante said. "We'll go with that."

"It'll be here in ten days," The Gunman said.

"Ten days?" I said. "That's too long."

The Gunman just repeated himself. "Ten."

"Why's it take so long?"

"We're not delivering patio furniture," the man said, patting the sectional for emphasis.

I gestured at the house. "Do you have anything we can just buy now?"

"I don't hold inventory," he said. "I'm not a warehouse."

"Nothing?"

"I have seven grenades that weren't picked up yesterday."

"How much?" Dante asked.

"Six hundred each. Forty-two hundred for the box."

"Who didn't pick them up?" I asked.

"That's confidential," The Gunman said.

"We have plenty of money," I said to Dante. "Let's get them."

"Would be nice to have some grenades again." He looked up at the sky, then started to nod his head. "All right, fine. So how much do we owe you today, then?"

"Twenty-five percent now, seventy-five percent later."

"I know that. Do the math for me."

The Gunman didn't hesitate. "Six thousand seven hundred. That's the down payment of two thousand five hundred for the guns and ammunition, but the full four thousand two hundred for the grenades."

Dante dug into his pocket and counted out the money he'd grabbed from the office. "Here."

The Gunman slipped the money inside his vest.

"Anything else for you two?"

"Nah. We're good."

The Gunman smiled but not at either of us. "Follow me, then." He snatched up his fillet knife and escorted us to the garage, where he pointed at a cardboard box. "Seven grenades."

Dante inspected the contents. "Looks good."

"I appreciate you coming here." The Gunman pressed the garage door opener on the wall. "Goodbye."

I set my water glass on some random shelf after Dante had picked up the box, and we walked out, the front gate opening automatically.

"Why couldn't we drink the water?" I asked after we had gotten into the truck.

"He drugs it. Thinks it's funny."

"Why do you even go to him?"

"No one else around. And Ingeniero likes him."

"I don't."

"Neither do I," Dante said as we drove away.

XIX

The Boy

The Aztecas went on the attack the next day. Maybe they knew our supplies were low. Maybe they were just pissed about not getting Salas. Either way, though, it didn't matter. They were shooting up everything, and we couldn't do shit about it, because a box of grenades didn't do you any good if by the time you picked yourself off the floor, the Aztecas were already gone.

We took to hiding. But that was even worse. I had gotten really twitchy and jumpy since Salas, and I could barely sit for five minutes before the anxiety pulled me out the hole I was hiding in. I'd leave my house and go to the tattoo shop. I'd leave the tattoo shop for my house. Then I'd sit for a few minutes before hurrying over to Carlos's.

Every car was following me. Every guy on the corner was watching me. Everyone was waiting to signal the sicarios to come racing around a corner on their bikes and gun me down.

So I took to the mountains, a place where I could roam and wander and keep watch of everything around for miles, baking in the sun but getting the dread off of me.

Then Carlos would call: "They got another last night. Not even AA this time. Just some taxi driver and his kid. Executed them both."

I didn't know why he was telling me.

"You hear about Angel's younger brother? Got him too."

I just rode around, stopping on hilltops, watching, breathing, waiting, then heading off again.

Somewhere far from the city, farther than the mine I had explored a couple of times, I found a shack, dull red and splintered with litter piled up against its sides like it was a dumping ground for people to empty out their cars on their way to someplace else. For a moment, I thought maybe it was an outhouse, but as I got closer, the litter became trinkets and vases of dried flowers and bottles of unopened alcohol next to small bow-tied presents. I stopped. Over the door, a plaque read, "Santa Muerte."

There was no handle or knob on the door, but I still knocked. When nothing happened, I pushed it open, and a wave of hot, sour air rolled out.

I leaned closer, tipping my bike, getting a look into the darkness. There were unlit candles that'd sunk in on themselves from the heat. And more trinkets. And clothes. And fruit in various stages of decay. Most everything was heaped at the feet of a skeleton against the back wall, dressed in a dirty gray cloak. It had a black wig with a crown of plastic flowers. A rusted scythe had fallen from its hand and lay near a half-deflated, peeling soccer ball.

I got off the bike and stepped inside. I put the scythe back in Santa Muerte's hand, and for the first time in days, I actually wanted to sit and stay somewhere for a little bit.

The floor was just the desert sand, and I lowered myself into it at the foot of the figure. My heart was pounding, but I felt safe. Inside the dim, hushed hut, I felt protected.

Around me, scattered among the gifts, half-buried in the sand, were bills in various denominations. I took some money from my own pocket and buried it in the ground, hoping it was enough to appease the saint.

The Aztecas were coming, I told Santa Muerte, and I needed her protection.

XX

The Sicario

Me and my brother were sitting out on our patio. It was dark. We were the only ones home, our parents and little sister off on another vacation. I put our friend Jonathan on the speaker and set my phone on the glass table.

"The Beast," I told the trafficker as I grabbed my drink.

"I know that," Jonathan said. "What's his real name?"

I sat back and crossed my arms. "Shit if I know."

"Oh, come on. Nobody said anything?"

I looked to Nemesio, and he leaned over the phone. "They all just call him The Beast."

"Did you even *ask* what his real name was?"

"They didn't know it."

Jonathan sighed. "You didn't ask. Okay. Whatever. What else did you find?"

"Big kid," Nemesio said.

"No shit."

"*Really* big."

"You saw him?"

"In the flesh."

"Could you take him?" Jonathan asked.

"Yeah. Why would you even ask that?"

"Because he's big, and you're small. It's a serious question."

Nemesio got even closer to the phone. "We're not small."

"I'm not insulting you," Jonathan groaned.

"Yeah, you are."

"You want me to insult you, you little Gizmo gremlin? How's that?"

"You're the gremlin, you 'roid monster," Nemesio yelled.

Jonathan must've pulled the phone away from his mouth, because he said something, but it was hard to hear. Maybe he was swearing at us. He came back clearer. "Listen—"

"And I haven't even stopped growing, so go fuck yourself." Nemesio got up from the table and paced around behind me just beyond the light of the patio.

The phone was silent.

I said, "Hey. We haven't seen this kid in about a week, so it doesn't even matter. He's gone. Like BB. Vanished."

"He's not gone," Jonathan said. "The Aztecas and AA are fighting. He's laying low."

"Fine. We'll wait."

"I'm not waiting," Jonathan said. "He has a family, doesn't he?"

"Sure. Couple sisters. His mom. His grandma."

"Could you get to them?"

"What's that supposed to mean?" Nemesio asked, darting back to the table.

"I'm just asking a question, for Christ's sake."

"We could get to them." I looked at Nemesio. "Right?"

He nodded and pushed away from the table. "Right."

"Then hear me out, okay?" Jonathan waited a moment, but Nemesio and I didn't say anything, so he just went on talking. "His sisters. Take them. *Take*, not kill," he said. "Do not kill them. Just take them. Okay?"

"Yeah, sure. Don't kill them," I said.

"Take them *where*?" Nemesio asked.

"I don't know," Jonathan said. "I don't care. Just find a place to stick them for a couple days. I'll get something set up with The Beast. Get him to come to you. How's that?"

"We don't need the help," Nemesio said.

"Would you just chill?"

"*You* chill."

I hit Nemesio on the arm, then asked Jonathan, "When do you want this done?"

"The sooner, the better."

"Could go get them tonight."

"Do it," Jonathan said before disconnecting.

I looked at Nemesio and grinned. "Hermanos de la Muerte."

XXI

The Boy

I tried to fall asleep, but I could only lie there in the office, silence all around me, rolling side to side. My mind, even in the middle of the night, wouldn't let up. I replayed the conversations I'd had with my mom, my sisters, my grandma, Carlos, Ingeniero, Dante, everyone, and none of this was making any sense anymore. I hadn't made anything better. Everything was falling apart.

And I had no clue how to fix it.

I finally just gave up on sleep and moved to the desk, crossing my arms over the top of it and resting my chin on my wrists.

But the more I sat there, the more I wanted to head out and just ride around, looking for something to just change everything back to how it was. Forget making anything better.

I started to get up, but froze when the door to the tattoo shop below me opened.

Or at least I thought it had. I held my breath and listened.

Maybe someone was coming through the shop to the back staircase. Maybe there were footsteps. Quiet footsteps.

I tried to tell myself that it was Dante or Carlos, but I was also telling myself that my gun was on the pallet in front of the couch, too far to grab. But the other, the black Beretta Dante had gotten me, was in the desk, in the middle drawer on my right.

A board creaked. One of the warped steps.

My eyes swung to the door while my hand went for the side of the desk and felt around. As the tips of my fingers found the cold metal of the drawer handle, the door popped open. Two little balls or rocks or something came rolling in, and the door shut.

The little objects wobbled across the uneven wood.

Santa Muerte flashed through my mind, and I dropped to the floor, taking cover behind the desk as the grenades exploded with sharp, deafening cracks, shaking the floorboards and peppering the desk and the map of Juárez with splinters.

Two men yelled out, and the door got kicked in. The office lights flicked on. Footsteps rushed in.

But then they paused.

One of the men said something, and the other answered. They were processing my absence.

They knew I was there, though. It wouldn't take them long to find me. It was just the desk and the couch, and the sicarios had to be right beside the couch, staring down at the indented cushions, but now turning to the desk.

I yanked open the drawer and grabbed the gun. I'd get them before they could get me, but before I could even pop up, the sicarios opened fire, canvassing the desk with bullets. I dropped to the floor, the gun clutched to my chest.

They should've waited another half a second. They should've waited until I'd actually shown myself. They would've had me if they'd waited, but they were too anxious, excited, or whatever, and screwed themselves. I just had to lay there as the thick oak desk absorbed their spray.

One of them reloaded and then started firing again.

I turned over onto my stomach and wormed my way to the side of the desk, peeking around it. The sicarios, dressed in black, holding AK-47s, looked like they had on bullet-proof vests, so I aimed at one of them just above the chest and fired three quick shots. The guy dropped his gun and grabbed his neck. I shot him again, this time in the leg, and he collapsed. His partner turned to me as I went squirming back to safety behind the desk, several rounds hitting the floorboards where I'd been.

I turned on my back, staring at the wooden beams above me, pistol gripped tight.

The sicario stopped shooting, and everything got quiet. Everything except for his partner who I'd hit in the neck. He was choking and bubbling and coughing.

I aimed my gun toward the top edge of the desk, ready to shoot the head that leaned over it. Except nothing happened. I looked down at my feet, at one end of the desk, then up at the other. Nothing. It was a waiting game now, and I was trapped, pinned in the back of the office.

So I just went for it. I turned myself over, scrambled to my knees, and hopped up from behind the desk.

The first few shots were blind, me just pulling the trigger, but then I spotted the sicario standing near the couch, a grenade in his hand, the pin pulled. He and I looked at each other, realized who had won, and I shot him twice in the face.

He went down in a heap.

The grenade rolled from his hand and came to rest against the other sicario still clutching his neck. I dove behind the desk, and there was one final pop.

~

Ten minutes later, after I'd messaged Dante and Carlos, they found me still crouched behind the desk in an office splattered with blood.

"Nobody's around?" I asked.

"It's clear," Dante said.

I pulled myself up into the desk chair and sighed.

Carlos stepped over to the sicario I'd shot in the neck and inspected his arm. "Lot of tattoos. Definitely Aztecas."

I was shaking my head. "I knew they were following me. I *knew* it."

Dante picked up one of the AK-47s but tossed it aside when he saw it'd gotten bent from the grenade. He grabbed the other, checked it carefully, then gave a satisfied nod.

Carlos ran a hand over the bullet holes in the desk. "Guess Javier knew what he was doing when he bought this thing, huh?"

"Let's go hit them back," I said.

"Sure."

"Now."

He shook his head. "We need our guns first."

"We can't wait."

"We have to wait."

"They'll do this again."

"Not if you stay low."

"I *was* staying low," I said.

"We can hang them," Dante offered. "You want to hang them?"

"Yeah," I said. "And with a note that says, 'This is what happens when you attack me.'"

"When you attack *The Beast*," Dante clarified.

I looked at the bodies, at the blood. The place smelled, and the air was too heavy. "I have to get out of here." I stood and circled the desk, grabbing the rifle from Dante. "I have to go."

"The clip's half-empty," Dante said.

"Better than nothing." I headed for the door.

"Watch your back out there," Carlos said.

I turned around. I looked at the bodies again. "I want to take the truck. I need to take the truck. Give me the keys."

"Where are you going?" Carlos asked.

"Who has the keys?"

"Why do you need the truck?"

"I'm going up into the mountains. I'm staying out there the rest of the night. Keys. Now."

Dante said, "So I'm supposed to walk home?"

"Take my bike. It's a push start." I held up my hand. "Keys."

Dante looked at the dead sicarios, then at Carlos, who shrugged.

"Give them," I said.

Dante sighed and tossed them over.

"And this is mine too," I said, hurrying back to the desk. I tore the map of Juárez from the wall and pulled Javier's black duffel bag from the hidden cubby hole. "Never coming back here," I said and walked out.

And by *here*, I meant Juárez, not the office. The duffel bag had a couple hundred thousand dollars in it, more money than my family would ever need.

I was going to take them to El Paso. I'd find someone to take us there, someone who wasn't Tomas, someone who didn't know Dante, or Carlos, or Ingeniero and wouldn't say a word about our crossing. Someone who would just let us disappear like so many others had from the city.

Down on the first floor, I poked my head out the shop door, scanned the street, then hurried to the Lobo, racing it up into the mountains and settling near the abandoned mine to wait until morning.

~

I came down from the mountains and stopped at a Superette for breakfast: an egg-and-bacon sandwich and a Jolt Cola. The newspapers stacked at the counter showed a headline announcing "A Day Without Death." It was the mayor's campaign promise. The city hadn't actually experienced anything close to it. But the mayor was trying to get people to buy into the idea, trying to buy into his vision. He wanted to become the city's first two-term mayor, and he had big plans. *If* elected.

It was all a dream. It was never going to happen. Not his re-election. Not the day without death.

Not that I cared. I was leaving.

And soon.

I stepped forward in the line.

It just wasn't going to be as quick as I'd hoped. I didn't know anyone who could take my family north, at least no one who Carlos and Dante, my guides in this world, didn't know. I'd spent all night thinking about it, but I realized I knew no one.

I paid for my breakfast and went to stand outside in the morning sun. There was a small wooden cross shoved upright in a crack in the sidewalk. Someone's name was written on it in white paint, and a wilting bouquet of flowers lay next to it.

Had anyone put something up for the guy in that green van?

A woman hurried along with two little girls at her side. A stray dog kept pace. The sun was just above the horizon, and their shadows were stretched frighteningly thin behind them.

The sandwich was gone in four bites, and the soda gone soon after. I climbed into the Lobo and went wandering the streets, turning randomly as the urge struck, trying to think how I might get my family out of the city.

A little while later, my phone started to vibrate in the cup holder. Someone, probably Carlos or Dante was calling, but I ignored it.

Maybe my family could just pile into the Lobo and race across the desert, blowing right through the border.

The phone buzzed with a message, then another, and another. I grabbed it to turn it off, but I caught sight of the first message.

Carlos had sent it.

Heard shots across the street.

I scrolled to the next one.

Checking your house.

And the next.

Where are you?

"Fuck." I was down on the southwestern edge of the city. I wasn't anywhere near my house. "Fuck, fuck, fuck." I raced over to the Periférica Camino Real Highway, taking corners at full speed, the tires sliding on patches of sand and clipping curbs and hitting potholes. The truck bounced and the metal and springs groaned.

I reached Joaquín Terrazas after only a couple minutes and jumped out of the truck before it'd even come to a full stop.

Carlos was outside my house. The front door was closed, untouched, and for a second, I thought everything was fine. My family was inside, sleeping, and it was fine.

"Shit, man," Carlos said. "I'm sorry, dude."

I rushed past him, reaching for the door.

"It's bad," he warned. "I don't know if you want to—"

I flung the door open, and the stench of gunpowder was strong.

But the smell of blood was stronger.

I went in, and on the floor in front of the couch, in

pools of dark purple-red, were Mom, Katie, and Grandma.

My knees gave out, and I collapsed, gasping, choking. My mouth opened as if to yell, but I couldn't draw the breath to make the sound. I just shook and stared at my family until my vision blurred, and they disappeared behind the tears.

I reached, trembling, and felt Katie's shoulder, her arm. She was warm. I squeezed her, hoping she would respond. "Katie? Katie?" I pulled away and dropped my face to the floor, my forehead hitting with a thud. I fell to my side and then, I finally screamed.

But where was Isa?

I bolted upright. "Isa? Isa!"

"I couldn't find her," Carlos said from the doorway.

"Find her." I scrambled on hands and knees to the bedroom, then pulled myself to my feet with the help of the doorframe. The small room was empty, so I hurried to the kitchen. Then the bathroom. Where was she? "Isa!" I searched the entire house again.

"I don't think she's here," Carlos said.

I ran out the back door, shielding my eyes from the rising sun, and twirling around, yelled, "Isa? Isa!"

Carlos stepped into the open doorway. "I looked. It took you so long to get here—"

"Shut up. What happened?" I grabbed him. "What'd you see?"

He shook his head. "Nothing. I was sleeping. I just heard some shots and—"

"How many?"

"I don't know. A few."

"And then what?"

"Nothing. Just quiet. I called. Messaged you. And came over."

My hands dropped from his chest. I turned and vomited my breakfast into the sand. The energy drink, still slightly carbonated, fizzed and turned the ground neon green. "Why wasn't I here?" I choked. "She would've protected them. She would've protected them."

"Who?" Carlos asked.

"Santa Muerte," I howled.

"That's crazy talk."

"Is it? Look at me. And look at them." I waved my hand at the house. "Look at me," I shouted, "and look at them!"

A siren was coming from down the ridge.

"Come on," Carlos said.

"No. Look at me," I mumbled as I stumbled into the house, "and look at them."

Their shoes were on the back door mat, and I fell against the wall, sliding down to the floor, exhausted. I picked up one of Katie's little black Mary Janes and clutched it, crying, crying until I became lightheaded.

I didn't move when the ambulance arrived. I didn't move when the police came and wrote down their notes. I didn't move as the bodies were carried away. And I didn't move when the house fell silent again.

Carlos, having stood by my side the entire time, knelt down. "We can find Isa," he said. "We can."

I reached up and clutched the edge of the counter with fingers wet from tears and pulled myself to my feet. Isa's red tiara was by the sink, shining in the sunlight, and I grabbed it. I opened the fridge, took out a vial of Isa's insulin, said, "She'll need this," and went shuffling away.

~

Carlos had to drive. I couldn't see anything clearly. We went around the barrio, stopping every halcon we saw, telling them to watch for my sister. I described her in as much detail as I could, giving each halcon a three-minute speech.

Carlos then stopped at her school, at the hospitals,

and whatever shelter we came across along the way. She wasn't at any of them, and no one had seen her.

"Don't know where else to go," Carlos finally admitted as we sat at a stop sign.

When I didn't say anything, he just rolled through the intersection and kept driving, circling blocks we'd already been on, driving down streets we'd already seen, then just ending up at the house on Calle Santiago, where Javier had killed BB and left Carlos and me to bury him in the backyard.

The metal chair was still on its side in the middle of the room. I set it upright and flopped down, facing the wall, my thoughts scattered and wild.

Carlos left me alone. He might not have even come inside. Maybe I heard the truck drive away. Maybe not. He could've just sat out there the whole afternoon. I wasn't paying attention. When I finally noticed him beside me, it was dark out, and he had a cardboard box in his hands. He held it out.

"What?" I mumbled, my lips dry and my cheeks stiff from the dried tears.

"Our grenades." He opened the box. "Let's go start a war."

I rubbed my eyes. "What?"

"The Aztecas. There's a house in Villas de Salvárcar that's having a party tonight. An Aztecas party. Come on." He hit me lightly on the shoulder. "Let's get them back."

I pushed myself up, my muscles aching, and followed Carlos to the Lobo. He set the box of grenades between us and pulled out four of them.

"Here. All you gotta do is pull the pin," he said, shaking them, making the metal rings jingle.

I took the hard plastic objects and laid them in my lap. I stared out the window. "I fucking hate myself."

Carlos just said, "Hate the Aztecas," and drove us to Salvárcar.

When we got to some dark side street on the other side of the city, Carlos pointed at a boxy sea-green house. A dull, steady bass came out of it and shook the Lobo. Through the barred windows, people were standing in groups, drinking.

"Aztecas," Carlos said, reaching into the box for some more grenades.

"Aztecas," I repeated, gritting my teeth, picking the grenades from my lap.

Four grenades.

For Mom. For Grandma. For Katie. For Isa.

Growling, I jumped from the truck and sprinted toward the house.

Nobody saw us coming.

I kicked open the front door, we pulled the pins, and rolled the grenades into the house. As they went bouncing across the floor and over feet, Carlos and I were already back at the truck, ready to race out of there.

But when the grenades went off, I didn't climb into the cab with Carlos. Instead, I just listened to the screams and cries. And I grinned.

I pulled out my pistol and went back. Amid the blood and body parts and broken glass, I found some guy who looked like he was going to survive and shoved my gun in his face, snarling, saying, "Bring her back. Bring Isa back. I won't stop."

XXII

The Sicario

The day after Nemesio and I shot up that family, I was sat down in a metal chair at a metal table in a windowless room across from a balding, beefy police chief. The guy's blue-and-white cap with its seven-pointed star staring back at me rested near his folded hands.

"So that's everything?" he asked.

"The whole story," I said.

"Uh-huh." The man sucked at something between his teeth.

I crossed my arms and let myself slide lower in the uncomfortable chair, pretending to be comfortable.

"So none of that was your fault?" the man asked.

I shook my head. Naturally, I had deflected all blame to the family for what had happened. They should've just listened to Nemesio and me. We weren't there to hurt them. But they'd tried to run. And then they'd tried to fight. I told the chief commissary that he should be very happy we had even gotten out of there with the little girl. "It was a mess, so crazy," I lied. "I almost shot her too. The little girl." I smiled. "Do you know how hard it is to kidnap someone? I mean, really, Miguel? I deserve some credit."

The man on the other side of the table curled his fat lips into a slight scowl. "You crossed the line with this."

I shrugged. "Not our fault."

"Who ordered the hit?"

"Wasn't a hit," I said. "Was a kidnapping."

"Which turned into three homicides and a kidnapping."

"Right."

"Who ordered it? Your friend in El Paso?"

"What friend?"

"You don't have a friend up there?"

"He's not my friend."

"You act like it by the way you're protecting him."

"Not protecting him. I'm protecting Nemes and my business."

"Sociopaths R Us?"

"Such a funny guy."

"You need to keep things clean. Especially when you're dealing with me, okay?"

"What do you care?"

"*Okay?*"

"That girl, whatever her name is—"

"Isa," Miguel said.

"—is being shipped to Denver, and when she gets there, you're going to be a hero. So what's the problem?"

Miguel shook his head, saying, "You shouldn't have killed that family," but I had seen the sparkle in his squinty brown eyes when I had said the word "hero."

I turned over my palms—"It happened, don't worry about it"—then grinned. "And how many traffickers have you caught over the last couple years because of me? Hmm? You're fucking Robocop. Going to be a fucking *legend.* How long has the FBI been trying to get this Denver guy?"

"Ten years."

"Yeah, a fucking legend."

"Where is Isa now?"

"Up in Angeles. Gave her to a coyote."

"I need to know when she's close to Denver."

"Yeah, don't worry about it. She'll be there in a few days. Middle of next week, maybe."

"Good." Miguel leaned back in his chair, crossed his arms, and stared at me. "You really look just like your father did when he was your age."

"I think my dad looks like a pedophile."

Miguel snorted at that, then motioned toward the door behind him. "All right. Get out of here."

I gave a salute and bounced out of the chair. "See ya when I see ya."

Outside, a rare rain cloud had just passed over the city, giving it a fresh, shiny look. The sun was working hard to dull the colors back to dust and powder, though. My dad's Mercedes was already dry and riddled with water spots.

I climbed in and called Jonathan. Meeting with Miguel was only half of my morning's business.

"Bad news, my friend."

He groaned. "Don't tell me that."

"We had to take out the family."

"Take out the family?"

"We went in all quiet and shit, but the old lady was up and she flipped. And then the mom had a knife under her bed. And then the girls were running around like lunatics." I paused for him to say something, but he didn't, so I added, "We had to."

"Goddammit," Jonathan said. "What's with you? First Herrera. Now these guys?"

"Kidnappings aren't easy. This isn't the movies. You can't just throw a bag over someone's head and shove them into a van. People fight. Every time."

"Hermanos de la *fucking* Muerte. You *really* live up to your goddamn name."

I had a sudden, terrible urge to tell Jonathan that Nemesio and I hadn't screwed up at all, that we were more competent than he could ever know, that we were playing this from so many angles that it'd blow his mind, but instead, I just said, "Yeah, well..."

If he knew that girl was alive, he'd get involved, try to get her back, and then he and Miguel would cross paths, and then it'd all go to hell. But this way, Miguel was happy, Nemesio and I were happy, and Jonathan was somewhat pissed. Good enough.

"You get any rain up there?" I asked.

"I'm not paying you," Jonathan said.

"Hey, whoa. Hold on."

"The whole point was—"

"To get The Beast, I know. We'll still get him."

"I'll believe it when I see it."

"Give it time. Give it a couple weeks."

"*Weeks?* No."

"The plaza's hot. Haven't you seen what's been happening?"

"It's always hot."

"We're lying low for a bit."

"Don't be little bitches."

I sat up. "Hey. We had a fucking firefight down the street from our house."

"There's firefights on every street down there."

"Not where we live. Not in—" I cut myself off before saying anything specific. Jonathan was Hermanos de la Muerte's best customer, but I wasn't telling him where we lived. Not in a million years. I said instead, "Not in our corner of Juárez."

"I'll find someone else, then."

"No one's doing this for you. Not now. Shit's blowing up. Bodies are dropping. Everyone's fired up." I chuckled, thinking that kind of sounded like a rap lyric from Dr. Dre.

Jonathan wasn't laughing. "Do your fucking job."

"How about you up our payment?"

"How about I give half a million to anyone that kills the two of you. How about that?"

"Jesus. I'm just messing with you."

"Kill that kid. Now."

"Fine. If it's that important, we'll go find him."

"Yeah. It's that *fucking* important."

"Okay, then," I muttered. "We'll do it. Hermanos de la Muerte."

XXIII

The Boy

After the grenade attack in Salvárcar, Carlos dropped me back off at the house on Santiago, where I crawled into a corner and sat until the sun came up. A spot of light shone through a hole in the sheet over the window and crept down the wall toward me. At some point, I must have reached into my pocket and pulled out the vial of insulin, because I was squeezing it in my palm, staring at the sun spot, when the Nokia phone started ringing. I didn't recognize the number but still answered.

"I heard what happened," Ingeniero said.

I sat up. "Can you help me?"

"You do something like that again, and I'll—"

"Like what?"

"That party."

"I'm looking for my sister. Help me find her."

"You need to calm yourself down."

"I have to find her."

"By bombing a group of teenagers?"

"Aztecas," I said. "We sent a message."

"That was no message."

"Fuck that. I'm finding Isa."

"Listen to me." He paused; I didn't say anything, so he went on. "What you have to do is *think*. Stop reacting, and think."

The spot of sunlight had reached the floor.

He asked, "Did you see my snake the other day?"

"The dried thing?"

"Yes. I've had that since I was a kid. It killed my dog. The snake, it's a viper, an Agkistrodon, and it bit my dog when we were out playing. I loved that dog, and I had to watch him die."

"So you killed the snake? Good."

"I tried to. The snake hid in its hole, so I went after it, but when I stuck my hand in, reaching and stretching, I got bit. Obviously, I survived, the snake had used all its venom on my poor dog so my fingers only swelled a little, but I learned a lesson. When I went back to the viper's hole the next morning, I waited. I stood there, an ax in my hands, and I waited. For three hours. I didn't move. I just waited until the viper finally came out. Its nose. Its eyes. Its head. Its body. And then, after three hours, I brought the ax down. And I cut off its head."

"I don't have time to wait," I said.

"You don't have time to let your emotions drive you," Ingeniero corrected. "Be patient."

I looked down at the spot of sunlight sneaking across the floor.

"Do we have an understanding?" Ingeniero said. "No more attacks."

"But there isn't time."

"Well, I cancelled your order with The Gunman, so there's time now. No more of this."

"What?" I clutched the insulin vial in my fist, then

punched the wall, putting a hole in the plaster. "We need those guns."

"Calm down," Ingeniero instructed.

"The Aztecas are going to kill us."

"They won't."

"The Aztecas have Isa."

"I don't think so. This has something to do with my friend in El Paso."

"Jonathan?"

"If you stop this horsing around, I'll look into it."

"Will you?"

"Will you calm down?"

"I'm going to find her."

"You put your hand in another viper pit, and you'll get bit. What happens then to your sister?"

"Then do something," I said.

"No more attacks?"

"Fine." I hung up.

The sun spot reached the etched chrome of my gun lying on the floor and made it sparkle like the jewels of a tiara.

I kicked the thing away.

~

There was no messaging, no sliding of the front gate, no greeting at the door. I just climbed over the security wall and dropped down into the yucca plants that were glistening from a recent rain.

The Gunman was in his kitchen eating breakfast at the island, his back to me, so I grabbed a large stone from the raked sandy patch in the corner of the yard and threw it through the glass door.

The Gunman jumped at the explosion, and I walked in.

We both looked at the knife, resting beside a bowl

filled with grapefruit. The Gunman reached for it, but I was quicker and flicked it away, sending it skittering over the edge and onto the floor.

Sighing, The Gunman rested his hands in his lap. "Yes?"

"My guns," I said.

The sweater-vested man shook his head, eyes down. "That order was cancelled."

"Not cancelled," I said. "We paid for them. We want them."

"You paid a deposit," The Gunman said. "I'll refund you."

"Screw that. Get the guns here."

"Even if I wanted to go against Ingeniero, why would I sell you anything after what you did last night?"

"They got what they deserved."

"What they deserved?"

"They killed my family."

"No one at that house killed your family," The Gunman said.

"They were Aztecas."

"They were kids. High school kids having a party."

"They were Aztecas," I repeated.

"No," The Gunman said. "They weren't."

I shook my head. "You don't know that. Get me my guns."

"Ingeniero cancelled the order."

I pounded my fist on the counter. "You want us all to die?"

He smirked. "Wouldn't be the worst thing to happen."

I shoved the man from his chair. "What do you have here? Give it to me."

The Gunman reached around the island and grabbed his knife, jabbing it in my direction. "You get out—"

I stepped back.

"—or I'll slice you open."

My hands balled into fists, ready to take him on.

The knife swished through the air. "Get out."

I turned and left the man there on the floor, but I didn't leave. I went down the hall and into the garage.

I had pulled everything off the shelves by the time The Gunman peeked through the door.

"I don't have anything," he said, scanning the mess of scattered tools and trash.

I grabbed a screwdriver and threw it at him, making him cry out as it stuck into the wall next to his head. "Get me my guns," I warned, "or you're dead."

"Kill me, and you'll be dead within the hour," The Gunman shouted as I walked out the side door of the garage.

~

I didn't go far, just to the truck that was parked down the block. I called Dante. "You hear about my family?"

"Yeah, man. Really sorry. That's just—"

"I need to go to El Paso. I need you to come with."

"El Paso? You leaving?"

"Jonathan."

"We're done with him. Ingeniero said—"

"Ingeniero said Jonathan went after my family. And you said Jonathan traffics kids, right?"

"Yeah."

"Then he knows what happened. He has Isa. We need to get him."

"Did Ingeniero say we could?"

"I'll pay you. Five thousand." I was looking at the duffel bag filled with cash on the passenger side seat.

"Five?"

"Five," I repeated. "And five more when we get Jonathan."

"Okay, yeah, sure, I guess."

"Call Tomas. Now."

"Sure. Give me a minute. I'll ring you right back."

I hung up and studied the street, making sure The Gunman wasn't trying to creep up on me while I waited. Things looked quiet, though. The homes all had security walls, each topped with sparkling razor wire. No way The Gunman was sneaking through yards to get close. Oddly enough, his was the only house that didn't have such protection, but after today, I was sure that would change. The next time I came by, I'd probably just run the truck through his front gate.

My phone rang. "Yeah?"

"There's a wrinkle. Tomas lost one of his agents at the border. She got caught in some DEA shit or something. Now they're checking *everything* going across."

"So we can't get through?"

"Not right now. The lady had millions in cash at her house from all the bribes she'd been taking. It's serious."

"I'll find someone else."

"Well, wait. Tomas has got tunnels. They're a little sketchy, but—"

"Let's go."

"You claustrophobic?"

"No. I've crawled through mines. I don't care about a tunnel."

"Cool. Tomas can go anytime, then."

"Now."

"Meet me at the warehouse? You remember the spot?"

I said I did, and sped off.

We all arrived at about the same time, and took Tomas's Nissan Altima to a spot on the east side of the city.

"Sorry for the hike," Tomas said as he drove. "I had one closer to you guys, but the border patrol found it last week. Filled it up with concrete. Was a good tunnel, too. She had a good run. Three years." He added, "But don't you worry. This one's good too. It's short. Only a couple hundred yards."

"So long as it's safe," I said.

"Oh yeah. No issues. Been sending Chinese migrants through. A lot coming from China these days. They pay up to seventy-five grand a head. You know that?"

"Shit," Dante said. "I'm in the wrong business."

"I don't get all that, of course," Tomas said. "The Chinese smugglers take most. Or not really *take*, I suppose. The migrants don't have that kind of cash, so the smugglers put them in their debt. Them and their families, and then they take a big cut every time the 'worker bee' sends money home." He looked around at a four-way stop, then turned right. "I'm guessing you'll be hearing about all this on the news soon. It's not big yet, but it will be. Sinaloa is building up their ties with the Triad." Tomas rolled down his window and pulled up to a gate, where he waved a plastic card at an unseen reader that caused the gate to slide away. "Welcome to Juárez's newest private community, Andalusia," Tomas said as we wound our way through freshly laid streets and half-finished homes with big sheets of plastic flapping in the wind. "I wish they'd put more of these communities up. Lot easier to build a tunnel when you've got this kind of activity around."

At a dead end where a few homes had been finished, each of them looking like the others, Tomas pulled into a garage.

"Who lives here?" I asked, eyeing the car next to us.

"No one," Tomas said. "That's a prop. Everything here is a prop."

And by everything, he meant the entire house. It was fully furnished. Couches, paintings, light fixtures, dishes, pillows, beds, everything.

In the dining room, Tomas asked for some help with the table set, so the three of us shuffled it over against the wall. He then pressed a toe into a floorboard in the center of the room, causing it to click and pop up. Underneath, there was a handle, and Tomas grabbed it with both hands. Grunting, he lifted up a huge square of the floor.

Dante and I looked down into the hole.

"Just a second." Tomas squeezed between us and climbed into the darkness. At the bottom, he flicked on a light. "Okay. All clear," he said, smiling up at us.

I looked at Dante, who said, "Five grand, right?" and I nodded.

~

We emerged on the other side of the border in another house.

"Again," Tomas said when we'd climbed up and were standing inside a closet, "all props." He opened the door to a fully furnished bedroom.

"You guys really sell it," Dante said, kicking aside some clothes lying on the floor.

"Hector's waiting," Tomas said, and guided us to the garage where his cousin sat in his green van with the bullet hole I (Dante) had put in it.

"Where's Jonathan?" I asked.

"He's been a little random lately." Hector looked at the clock on the dash. "At this time of day, though, he's probably at home."

"Which isn't the best spot to grab him," Tomas added.

"It's locked down," Hector confirmed.

"Don't care," I said. "We're going there."

Hector and Tomas looked at each other.

"Do it," I said.

Hector nodded and pulled out of the garage.

We took a road that cut along the edge of the Franklin Mountains, giving us sweeping views of both El Paso and Juárez. The homes perched on this hillside looked like palaces, and Dante pointed at one that had a statue on its terrace.

"Is that the Statue of Liberty?"

"That's her," Tomas said. "I've never been able to decide if she was put there to be inviting or denigrating."

"How about both?" Dante asked.

Tomas's phone started to ring, and he answered it, listening for a moment, then told Hector to pull over.

"Don't pull over," I said. "Why're you pulling over?"

Tomas held up his hand for me to be quiet. "Yeah, yeah," he said to the phone. "Yeah, okay. Bye." He turned around, telling me and Dante, "That was Ingeniero. He said he doesn't want you up here."

"What? How's he even know I'm here?" I looked behind us as if I expected to spot the man trailing us.

"No idea," Tomas said. "He wants you back, though."

I shook my head. "No. He thinks we're here for something else. We can stay."

Tomas put his hands up. "Hey, if Ingeniero wants you back, you got to go back."

"That was fun," Dante grumbled.

"We're not going back," I said. "Ingeniero's just being stupid."

"Turn around," Dante told Hector.

"We can't leave," I yelled. "We're already here."

Hector started to do a U-turn.

Dante sighed. "Ingeniero says—"

"Forget Jonathan, then," I yelled. "Just drive around. We can look for Isa. I'll tell you what she looks like."

"We have to—"

"Three and half feet tall. Skinny. Hair halfway down her back," I blurted out.

"We have to go," Dante said.

"Brown eyes. A birthmark on her cheek. Like a

sunburn."

"We're going back," Tomas reiterated.

"No. Look for her."

Hector was stepping on the gas now.

"No. We're staying. We're staying." I tried to unlock my door to jump out, but Dante reached over and pulled me back. "Let go!" I swung an elbow at Dante, knocking him back.

"Screw you," he cried, pulling his gun. He stuck it in my chest.

"Are you kidding?" I cried. "Is this for real?"

"It's real," Dante said, glaring at me. "Don't be stupid. Ingeniero wants us back, we're going back." He poked me with the gun. "Just be cool."

"You asshole."

Hector kept driving.

XXIV

The Boy

I wanted to kill Ingeniero. And Dante. And Tomas and Hector. But after being forced back to Juárez, I just wandered the city searching for Isa, telling myself that she was still there. Jonathan might've had something to do with it, but he hadn't gotten her out of the city yet.

Eventually, I started skirting the edge of some barrio that belonged to the Aztecas, where I came across a couple of dealers hanging out near a bus stop.

I pulled to the curb on the opposite side of the street. They jammed their hands in their pockets and stared back. They didn't look serious. Just a couple of joker dealers who had no clue who I was. One wore a patched-up jean jacket, and the other had a windbreaker with lightning bolts streaking down his chest.

I waved for them to come over, but they shook their heads. The one in the jean jacket motioned for me to cross the street instead, so I got out, waited for a car to pass, then went over to them.

"Twenty-five pesos," the dealer in the jean jacket said when I got close.

"For?" I asked.

"Heroin. It's all we got today." The dealer shrugged his shoulders. "You cool?"

I handed him some money. "Here."

He counted it, but once he realized I had given him 2,500 pesos, he asked, "What's this?"

"I want you to tell me something."

He cracked a thin smile. "About what?"

"I'm looking for someone, a little girl. Eight years old." I described my sister.

"Never seen her."

"You hear anything?"

The man looked at his dealer buddy in the windbreaker, who said, "Nope."

I took another 2,500 pesos from my pocket. "Keep an eye out for her."

The guy took my money. "Sure. That's cool."

I went back to the Lobo. A couple blocks away, I found some more Aztecas dealers and bribed them too. And some more after that. I ended up converting dealers into my halcones the rest of the night, and when the sun started to rise, and I didn't know where else to go, I went back to the house on Santiago to rest.

My dirt bike was outside, leaning against the house, and as I opened the front door, Carlos was coming in through the back.

"What's up?" he asked, setting a shovel against the wall. He was covered in dust and sweat.

"What're you doing?"

"Burying BB. The cover wasn't on tight. Coyotes got him."

"Is Dante here? I saw my bike—"

Dante came in, wiping his brow. He saw me and

said, "You didn't snap the lid tight. Thanks for that."

I just glared at him.

"What? You still mad about El Paso?"

"You went up to Paso?" Carlos asked, taking Dante's shovel and propping it next to his.

"Went to look for Isa," I said.

"And? Find anything?"

Dante snickered. "We were there for, like, two minutes."

"Could've stayed longer," I said.

"I don't think so. You pissed off Ingeniero."

"We could've stayed."

"Oh, bullshit."

"I would've stayed. You pulled a gun on me."

Dante laughed. "Yeah. After you took a swing at me."

"'Cause you're an asshole."

"I'm not taking heat from Ingeniero because of you."

"Fuck Ingeniero," I yelled. "My family is dead. Isa is missing. Fuck Ingeniero."

Dante stepped toward me, a stupid smirk across his face. "You go right ahead and 'fuck Ingeniero.' See what happens." He tried to push by me to get out of the kitchen, but I wouldn't move from the doorway. "Get the fuck out of my way," he said.

Shaking my head, I said, "I would've stayed."

"Then go back. I don't give a shit what you do." Dante pushed harder.

"I'm getting her back," I growled.

"Good for you."

He pushed me, and I pushed him.

"Fuck you," Dante spat, getting close enough that I could count the hairs of his thin goatee. "What's it even matter?" he said. "Girls disappear...all the time. Deal with it."

I grabbed him by the neck. His muscles tensed, and I pinned him against the wall. He tried to knee me in the crotch but missed, hitting the inside of my thigh, and I squeezed until his eyes bulged. "*You* deal with it," I hissed.

Dante clawed at my arms, and I pulled him from the wall, then smashed him back into it, knocking his head against the plaster. I did it again and again, leaving a larger, deeper indent with each thud. When his eyes rolled up into his head and he passed out, I let him fall to the floor.

"Did you just kill him?" Carlos asked from the other side of the room.

"He's still breathing." I grabbed the roll of duct tape we'd used to bind BB and wrapped Dante's wrists and ankles.

"What're you doing?" Carlos asked.

"I don't know. He's a fucker."

"You want to stick him downstairs?"

I ripped the tape from the roll. "Downstairs where?"

Carlos opened up what I had assumed was a closet door. "For special guests," he said, flicking on a light and revealing a wooden staircase.

"What's down there?" I moved to the top step, smelling the air coming up. Dust and rust and vinegar and gas.

"Just some shit for when we need to hold someone. Could put Dante down there if you want. Keep you from killing him maybe."

I knelt down, so I could see the entirety of the room below us. Two metal chairs that looked bolted to the concrete floor were in the very center of the space. And behind them in the corner was a stained mattress, a cracked sink, and a toilet crusted in black.

I gave a grunt, and we hauled Dante down into the basement, setting him in one of the chairs. Carlos grabbed a pair of handcuffs from a pile of boxes underneath the stairs and snapped one end to Dante's wrist and the other to the chair.

I gave Dante a light slap on the cheek. "You should be scared of me, not Ingeniero."

Carlos smirked. "You're going to be running this barrio someday."

I didn't say anything, just headed back upstairs, the steps croaking under my weight.

"Ingeniero tell you he cancelled our order?" Carlos asked, following me up.

"Yeah."

"We needed those guns."

"No shit." I went around the kitchen, opening the cabinets. "Where's some food. Is there anything here?"

"Some soda in the fridge," Carlos said. "But about those guns... I might have another way to get them. I know a guy who knows a guy who's a muni cop. Victor Tosdado. I'm meeting him in an hour. You want to come with?"

I nodded and opened the last cupboard. "There's nothing here."

"I know. Go grab something. You got time. I'll meet you at the Avenida de las Americas footbridge."

I put my hands on the counter and hung my head. "No. No food. I can't. I'm going to look for Isa some more."

~

I had to get some food, though. I had to eat, and I ended up at La Que Sabrosa Quesadilla, sitting at the same table Carlos and I had sat at two weeks earlier, where he had told me of his bee stings, where he'd told me how I should protect the barrio, help my family, take care of them. He had given me a hundred dollars, and I'd been so happy.

Now I couldn't stop shaking.

Isa hadn't had insulin for two days. Her blood sugar would be high, very high, and she'd be sick and confused and tired. I'd seen it happen before. Even though we were careful to ration the insulin, trying to make sure we never ran out, there were gaps. Sometimes, it was maybe a half day, but others, it was longer. Much, much longer. And she'd get so groggy. And nauseous. She had to be feeling like that right now as I sat there also feeling sick, poking at the quesadilla.

I rested my forehead in my hands, staring at the plastic tabletop. A drop of sweat came down my temple, shivered at the edge of my jaw, then fell.

I took a breath, counted to ten, then twenty before losing track in the thirties. With a snarl, I stormed off and got on my bike, which I'd taken back from Dante. I scoured the side streets and narrow alleys that I hadn't been able to check in the truck.

The hour I had until I needed to meet Carlos passed fast, though, and I found nothing.

At the footbridge, Carlos stood near the center with his contact, Victor. The city of Juárez was sprawled out behind them, the city of El Paso before them.

Victor leaned over the railing, trying to read a banner that'd been draped from the bridge as the traffic passed below, fluttering it.

When I got near, he stood up straight and said, "Quinceañera. Never understood those."

Victor was as large as me, if not larger, but he wore tight jeans and a crisp, checkered dress shirt that made him look smaller.

I glanced over the railing and read the colorful announcement by the proud parents of some teenage girl, and it struck me that Katie's birthday would have been today. She would've been eleven.

Victor rested against the rail, adjusting his sunglasses. "Anyway, sounds like you need some guns?"

A semi rushed by, pulling a curtain of air behind it, cooling us for a moment.

Carlos said, "We do."

Victor pointed north. "You're making them nervous."

"It's the Aztecas they should be worried about. We need those guns to stop the Aztecas."

Victor looked at me. "EPPD just got some new M4 rifles. An M4 for every officer. Over a thousand."

I shrugged. "And?"

"I can get you some of them if that's what you're in the market for."

"I'd take them," Carlos said.

"Need ammo too," I said.

Victor nodded. "Of course."

"How about a dozen?" Carlos asked.

"Sure."

"When?"

"How's this evening sound?"

"Shit. That's awesome." Carlos slapped me on the shoulder.

"How much?" I asked.

Victor didn't think for long. "Let's say an even thirty grand."

"Damn. Expensive," Carlos said. "The Gunman's, like, a third of that."

Victor smiled. "Buy from him, then."

"We'll take them," I said, staring north at El Paso, scheming.

XXV

The Trafficker

The park across from my office building was one of those weird triangular bits of land leftover when two streets that don't run parallel converge. It was called Aztec Calendar Park, and it wasn't a nice park, just a concrete island with some decorative strips of colored rocks and a few ash trees. A circular stone monument, an ugly replica of the Aztec calendar (hence the name), lorded over the tiny island.

I was crossing through this, my ham-and-cheese sandwich from the corner bistro in hand, when someone called out to me from over by the calendar.

I stopped and turned. "Well, fuck me."

Ingeniero's enforcer, a brute of a boy, was glaring at me. He held up his hands, palms open. "No one's here. Just me."

He looked like shit: tired, beaten, desperate, and unarmed (as far as I could tell). Just a plastic tiara in his hand. I didn't know what to make of that, but whatever he was planning, I didn't need to be too worried. One block to the east was the county clerk's office, the city's detention facility, and the El Paso Police Department.

"You come to apologize?" I called out.

"You went after my family," the enforcer said.

I nodded. "And you came after me." This kid had eight inches and thirty pounds on me. I looked at the police station behind him. There were four squad cars parked outside. No officers in sight, though.

"Where's my sister?"

"Your sister? *Where?*"

"Isa," the enforcer said. "Where is she?"

"What do you mean?" I asked.

The Beast stepped toward me, snapping, "Where is my sister?"

"Hold on." I lifted the sandwich bag like it might protect me. "You don't know where she is?" I was thinking about the call I'd had with Alvaro. He'd said he'd killed the whole family. The girl should've been with the others, yet here I could see in this kid's eyes that his sister hadn't been there. Alvaro, the little asshole, hadn't told me the whole story. "I can't fucking trust anyone."

The kid said, "What?"

"Hermanos de la Muerte. They killed your family. They have your sister."

The tiara in the kid's hands went from a circle to an oval as he squeezed it, popping one of the jewels from its glue. It went rolling across the pathway, glittering in the sun.

"Alvaro and Nemesio Davilo," I said. "They're Hermanos de la Muerte."

"Davilo," the kid repeated. "Where are they?"

"Don't know. They live somewhere over by Club Campestre Juárez."

"What do they look like?"

"Sorry, kid. I've never met them. Ask around.

Hermanos de la Muerte," I said, emphasizing the last bit. "Maybe ask your boss. Ingeniero should know."

The boy grimaced. The tiara looked ready to snap in two.

I said, "You got a phone?"

The kid's brow drooped. "Huh?"

"You got a phone on you?"

He stopped squeezing the tiara. "Yeah."

I gave him the number of my burner, then said, "When you get those brothers, they're not going to tell you the truth. Not right away. You have to hurt them. Call me if you need."

The kid was just glaring at me, or maybe spacing out at nothing. It was hard to tell, but after a moment of him just breathing and shaking, he turned and walked away.

I left the triangle park too, smiling. When I got up to my office, I laid the sandwich on my desk and gave Ingeniero a call.

XXVI

The Boy

I climbed out of Tomas's tunnel and shoved the furniture back as I had found it. I kept repeating *Hermanos de la Muerte, Hermanos de la Muerte* as I walked away from the fake dining room. My phone chimed with a missed call from Ingeniero.

I rang him up, but before I could even say *Hermanos*, he cut me off.

"Salas wants to meet with you."

"Salas?"

"You're going to Sinaloa. Your flight is this evening at seven."

I stopped at the back door, staring through the glass at my bike on the patio. "I can't go to Sinaloa."

"I'm not asking you; I'm telling you."

"I'm looking for Isa. Hermanos—"

"No, you're going to Sinaloa."

"Hermanos de la Muerte took Isa. They—"

"Who?"

"Hermanos de la Muerte," I repeated.

"Who gave you that name?"

"What's it matter?"

"Sounds made up," Ingeniero said.

"It's not."

"I've never heard of them."

"Maybe 'cause you don't know everything like you think you do."

Ingeniero didn't speak for a moment, then said, "You go see Salas."

"You find anything on Isa? You said you'd look into that."

"I'm still looking."

I groaned. "Why are you so worthless?"

"Go see Salas," Ingeniero barked.

"No."

"If you reject this invitation, I will send someone to drag you there," Ingeniero warned. "And then your meeting will go very differently."

"I'm not going. I can't."

"He just wants to thank you for saving his life."

"I'm not leaving until I find Isa."

"Don't make me look bad."

"Help me find Isa, and then I'll go."

Ingeniero swore, said, "Be at the airport at seven," then hung up.

"Asshole."

I dialed up Carlos.

"Hey," he said. "You calling about Dante?"

"What about Dante?"

"Oh, I let him go. He promised to be cool. I told him to pick up the M4s from Victor later, so he'll stay out of your hair."

"Do you know Hermanos de la Muerte?" I asked.

"Heard the name, yeah. What about them?"

"I snuck back through Tomas's tunnel. Talked to Jonathan."

Carlos laughed. "Good on you."

"Ingeniero says he's never heard of them."

"That's hard to believe."

I stepped out of the house. "This all fucking sucks."

"Hey, man. You'll get through it. We'll find your sister. You've got a lead now."

"What do I do with it?"

"You know who might know something about them?"

~

Victor and I stood shoulder to shoulder on the footbridge, looking north at El Paso once again.

"Nineteen sixty-eight Dodge Charger," Victor said as the car passed under us.

I didn't say anything.

"Not a car guy?"

I pointed at a black truck with tinted windows. "Ford Lobo."

This time Victor didn't comment.

"What'd you find?" I asked.

Victor pulled a few pieces of paper from his pocket, unfolded them, then handed me the top one, a printout of a family portrait. "Meet the Davilos," Victor said.

They were lined up against a stone railing on a patio overlooking a golf course. The mother was wearing a white summer dress and the father a pale suit and tie. Their children, a daughter and two sons, stood dressed in blue to match their father's tie and the lace trim of their mother's dress.

"The boys are Hermanos de la Muerte," Victor said. "That's Alvaro, and that's Nemesio."

"They're little kids," I muttered.

"They're just short," Victor corrected me. "Really, really short."

At the bottom, Victor had handwritten 9109 *Calle Francisco de Urdiñola.*

"That's their home address," he said. "It's over in San Pablo on the other side of 45."

I gestured at the rest of the papers in his hands. "What's that?"

"More photos," he said, handing them over. "Some pictures I pulled from the internet."

"The internet?"

"Just something new with computers. People use it to chat with each other."

I flipped through the printouts, which were mostly shots of Alvaro and Nemesio staring seriously into the camera. "You know anything else about them?" I asked.

"Like what?"

I shrugged. "How to make them talk."

"The M4s are coming. Be here tonight. Stick one of those in their faces and see how they react."

"I guess."

"Otherwise, torture seems to work for you guys, doesn't it?"

I nodded, said, "Thanks for the help," and left.

XXVII

The Sicario

I was stretched out on a lounge chair in the backyard, going through some photos I'd gotten developed, trying to find something good to put up on my GeoCities site. Nemesio sat with a newspaper at the table, reading through Liga MX match scores. Every so often a ball would thump against the cement wall that surrounded our yard, and one of the neighbor kids would cheer as if he'd just scored a goal.

"So fucking annoying," Nemesio kept saying.

One of the kids gasped, and we both looked up. A yellow soccer ball was sailing over the top of the wall, over the razor wire. It came down and rolled up against my chair.

"Serves 'em right," Nemesio said, dropping his head back into the sports scores. "Hey, did Luis say anything about that girl?"

"Nope." It'd been like three days since we'd killed The Beast's family and taken his little sister to Luis's house on Calle Tabaco. No word since. I reached down and picked up the ball.

"Luis is such a troll. Where'd he say he was taking her across?"

I drew my arm back, ready to toss the ball over the wall. "Same place he takes them all. Anapra."

One of the neighbor kids yelled for the ball in a way that sounded a little too demanding, and I changed my mind about throwing it back.

"Anapra's a shithole. Why's he even like that place?"

"'Cause of the train tracks," I said. Anapra colonia, the poorest section in the whole city, was shoved off in the northwest corner of Juárez, where there was a freight line that ran parallel to the border for a quarter of a mile. It made so much noise and vibration that traffickers like Luis didn't have to worry about the border patrol's sensors detecting the people they shipped through the tunnels. The trains also made the tunnels more prone to collapse, of course, but that wasn't Luis's problem. He had plenty of tunnels up there in Anapra. If one collapsed, he just moved to another.

"Please," one of the kids finally called out.

I chucked the ball back, and waited for a thank you, but it never came. "Ingrates."

"Atlante won again," Nemesio said. "They might win the Apertura this year."

"They don't have the depth. Just a temporary hot streak."

"I don't know. They're looking pretty—"

The yellow ball flew over the wall again and hit Nemesio.

"You little shits." He grabbed the ball, and as they kids yelled out again, whining, "Please, please, please," he carefully tossed the ball into the razor wire.

The kids screamed in dismay, and Nemesio smiled.

"I actually thought about doing that the first time, but they said please."

Nemesio got up. "I'm going to the store for some Coke. You want anything?"

I shook my head and went back to my pictures.

Before shutting the patio door, Nemesio asked, "So where's Luis now?"

"No idea," I said. "Like I said, haven't heard squat. I assume he got the girl across, and she's with that Mike guy in Sunland Park now."

"Mike Arabit?"

I nodded. "He'll probably hole up at the racetrack for a day. Then he'll head up I-10."

"And when do we get paid?"

"Once she's in Denver."

"We should go to the Apertura Final."

"So long as it's just us. No Dad."

"Buy our *own* box seats this year."

"The Hermanos de la Muerte box."

XXVIII
The Boy

I called Carlos before I'd even reached the bottom of the
pedestrian bridge. "We're going after Hermanos de la
Muerte. Right now."

"Victor came through?"

"He gave me their address."

"Sweet."

I jumped on my bike. "Meet me where you hanged
Javier."

"Benito Juárez Plaza?"

"Get April and Ashley too."

"And Dante?"

"No. Leave him out of this."

I raced my bike down Calle Malecón to the plaza,
only waiting a couple of minutes before Carlos pulled up
with April and Ashley in the Lobo. I showed them all the
Davilo family portrait.

"Who's Hermanos de la Muerte? On the right?"

Carlos asked.

"Alvaro and Nemesio," I said, pointing.

"Got it." Carlos sped off.

I gave April and Ashley the rest of the printouts.

"Which one we going after?" Ashley asked.

"Whichever one we can get."

April unzipped a duffel bag lying between her feet, showing me the AR-15s.

"*Alive*," I said. "They know where Isa is."

"Well, that's good," April said, "because we're basically out of ammo."

"We're getting M4s tomorrow," Carlos said.

"I know. You told us."

Ashley tapped me on the arm. "Carlos said you'd give us five grand for helping. Is that right?"

I didn't remember who I'd promised what to, but I said, "Yes. And fifty when we get Isa."

"That's so cool." Ashley dug into the duffel bag and pulled out some rolls of duct tape.

My hands were sweating (and probably shaking too, but I was fidgeting so much I couldn't tell).

As we got closer to San Pablo, the city blocks got nicer, and the homes around us grew in size. The yards turned green and neat.

"Jesus," April muttered as we passed a massive iron gate flanked by towering palm trees and blooming red shrubs. Beyond it, an evergreen-lined driveway led away to a house of columns and granite.

"That's not a house," Ashley said. "It's the country club."

"Rich people."

Carlos turned down a narrow street, where the asphalt became primly laid brick that gently rattled the truck. "Calle Francisco?"

I looked at Victor's handwritten address. "9109 Calle Francisco."

"Let's see what we've got."

I unbuckled my seat belt and leaned forward. "That's it," I said, pointing at a low-slung, cream-colored house with a blue-gray tiled roof.

April let out a disappointed sigh. "It's the smallest house on the block."

"Still better than anything any of us will ever have," Ashley grumbled.

"Keep going," I told Carlos, so he continued down the block, turned around at the end of the cul-de-sac, and parked, facing the house.

"There's no wall or fence or anything out front," April said.

"Well, where would you even put it?" Ashley asked. "Their house is right up against the street."

"And sandwiched between their neighbors," Carlos added.

"We can just walk right up to it. Do you want to? Just go break the door down?" April asked.

"Wait," I said. "Just wait."

"For what?"

"Until one of them comes out. You don't stick your hand down a snake hole. You just wait until the snake comes out."

Carlos settled into his seat. "Works for me."

I reached my hand around the seat—"Give me a gun"—and flexed my fingers until April pressed an AR-15 into my palm. I set the rifle across my lap and watched, my eyes moving from the front door to the garage, then back.

The rest of the street, the palm trees, the neighbors, the cars, I ignored, and for the next hour, the sun beat down on us, warming the truck until we were all soaked in sweat.

But eventually, a white Mercedes turned into the cul-de-sac and paused outside the brothers' house. The garage door started to lift.

"Who's that?" April asked. "I can't see inside the

car. The reflection."

"Looks like the driver's short. Could be a brother," Carlos said.

The Mercedes turned into the garage.

"I'll go," Ashley said.

"Go where?" Carlos asked.

"Knock on the door." She set her rifle aside and pulled out a pistol from the duffel bag. "Someone's obviously home now," she said, tucking the pistol away. "Let's see who it is."

"Seriously?"

"Hey. I'm not sitting here for another hour. It's too hot."

"So if one of them answers the door, then what?" Carlos asked.

"You guys grab him." She pointed at the house. "Stand by the door. Just off to the side."

"And if no one answers?"

"People always answer the door for a pretty girl." She smiled.

"I don't know."

"Just let her go," April said. "It's fucking roasting in here. I'm going to faint."

I looked at Carlos.

"Sure, why not?" he said.

I lifted the AR-15 to my chest and nodded.

~

The front door was a double-wide made of slick black wood. Ashley looked left at Carlos and April, then right at me before reaching out and ringing the doorbell.

I took a breath and held it, listening. Our truck was at the curb, its engine running, the back door open, ready for us to throw Nemesio or Alvaro inside.

Ashley rang the doorbell again.

I squeezed my hands around the grip of the rifle, my finger twitching across the trigger.

The door lock disengaged with a heavy clack, and the door cracked open.

Ashley looked down and cocked her head. "Oh, hi," she said. "Is your—"

I jumped in front of her and shoved my rifle into the gap. The brother I was expecting to see wasn't there, though. It was just the little sister staring up at me, her eyes wide. I froze. "Shit."

Ashley squeezed around me and grabbed the girl by her flowery shirt and forced her way into the house.

The girl screamed, a pitchy, squealing whine.

"Shut up. Where's your brother?" Ashley demanded.

No more than a second later, Alvaro came rushing around the corner. "What's—" He stopped hard, his socks slipping on the tiled floor. His hands went up. "Whoa, whoa. Take whatever you want."

I lurched past Ashley and the little girl, and jammed the AR-15 into Alvaro's gut.

"Whatever you want," the brother cried. "Please. Christ."

I grabbed the back of his neck and threw him outside, sending him tripping over the front steps and sprawling onto the sidewalk, where April pounced on him, wrapping his wrists with duct tape.

I took a quick look around, saw nobody else in the house, and hurried out, calling to everyone, "Let's go. Get him up, and let's go." I reached down to grab Alvaro.

Behind me, the little girl shrieked, and a shot rang out.

Alvaro's face went white.

I spun around. "Don't hurt the girl."

Ashley hadn't. She'd shot Nemesio, who'd popped out of hiding somewhere. He was lying on the entryway floor, clutching a bloody shoulder, with his sister kneeling at his side, whimpering.

I rushed back inside. "Take this." I shoved my rifle into Ashley's hands.

"Get away from me," Nemesio grumbled as I lifted him to his feet.

His sister scooted backward across the floor and crawled under a hallway table.

"Stay there," I told her before half carrying, half dragging Nemesio away.

April and Carlos had already put Alvaro into the backseat of the truck. April was holding the door open, waiting for Nemesio, but instead of throwing him in, I shoved the brother against the side of the truck and pulled the Beretta from under my shirt, jamming the gun against his head.

His yellow polo shirt was darkening with blood where the bullet had passed.

I didn't need both brothers. And if I shot Nemesio right there in the street outside their home, I could probably get the information out of Alvaro even faster.

But before I could pull the trigger, Carlos grabbed Nemesio and flung him into the truck.

~

Somewhere along the way, Alvaro pissed himself, bringing a new stench to the blood and sweat that filled the truck. Neither of the brothers spoke, their mouths had been taped over, and none of us chose to speak, so we all just sat in silence as Carlos rushed us to the house on Santiago. He swung the Lobo around the back, maybe over the spot where BB had been buried, and we dragged the brothers down into the basement.

"Where're the handcuffs?" I asked as I threw Nemesio into a metal chair.

"Under the stairs," Carlos said, dumping Alvaro into the other one.

"Got 'em," Ashley said.

We cuffed the brothers to the chairs and stepped back, watching them dart their eyes around, probably trying to understand how everything had changed so quickly.

"Fucking pathetic," I said.

Ashley ripped the tape from the brothers' mouths. "How's it going?" she smirked.

I walked up to Nemesio and stuck my finger in the bullet hole near the top of his shoulder, making him wail. "Where is she?" I said. "Where is my sister?"

"Jesus," he groaned. "I don't know."

I dug my finger deeper into his shoulder, and he screamed.

"Stop. Please," Alvaro shouted.

I stepped over to the other brother and pointed my bloody finger in his face. "You're Hermanos de la Muerte?"

The asshole was quiet.

"Don't fuck with me," I said, reaching for Nemesio's shoulder again.

"Yes," Alvaro quickly said.

"And you killed my family?"

"We didn't kill anybody."

Behind me, Carlos said, "Oh, fuck you."

I stuck my finger into Nemesio's shoulder again, hooking the muscle, making him howl.

"We had to," Alvaro yelled. "We didn't want to, but we *had* to."

I jerked my finger out of Nemesio's shoulder and stared at Alvaro.

He tried to give a half smile. "We *had* to."

I punched him in the face, breaking his nose. "My sister. Isa. Where is she?"

Alvaro started choking on the blood pouring from his nose.

"Where is she?" I yelled.

"We never saw her," Nemesio finally spoke. "She wasn't there."

"Bullshit," I growled, punching him in the shoulder. "Fuck."

"She wasn't there," Alvaro repeated, drops of blood flicking from his lips and landing on my arm.

I turned to him. "You're lying. Where is she?"

"I don't know," Alvaro shouted, making himself choke on his own blood again.

"You fucking know. You know!" I spun away and circled the basement, past Carlos and Ashley and April. My hand went into my pocket, where I still had Isa's insulin. "Carlos? BB had a needle in his pocket? What'd you do with it?"

"Nothing," he said. "Probably still upstairs on the floor."

"Get it."

As Carlos went bounding up the stairs, I turned back to the brothers: Nemesio sweating, hyperventilating, and grimacing, and Alvaro trembling, unable to look at anything other than the floor between his feet.

"Talk," I said. "You better talk."

But they wouldn't, so when Carlos came back and handed me the syringe, I asked a new question.

"You know about insulin?" I stuck the needle through the top of the vial. "Isa needed insulin every day," I said. "It kept her blood sugar normal"—I filled the syringe—"but she couldn't take too much. Like this." I held up the syringe. "This is too much. It would've killed her. It'd kill anyone."

The brothers stared at me. I smiled, then lunged forward and jabbed the needle into Alvaro's stomach, injecting the insulin before he could react.

"What the fuck?" he cried. "Oh, come on, man, what the fuck?"

I leaned close. "You're going to start feeling really, really sick, you little fucker. You'll feel like throwing up. You'll get shaky and sweaty. And then you won't be able to think straight. Couple minutes after that, you'll go into a coma."

"We didn't fucking see her," Nemesio yelled.

"Maybe we missed her," Alvaro admitted. "Maybe we missed her. Get this stuff out of me."

"I don't believe you. Either of you," I shouted. "I would've found her. If she was hiding, I would've found her. But...she...wasn't...there!" I stuck the needle back into the vial, drawing out more of the insulin. "Nemesio?"

"We took her. We took her," he finally admitted.

"Where?" I yelled, shaking the syringe.

"Help him," Nemesio pleaded, looking at his brother. "Give him the antidote or whatever."

"Tell me where she is."

The brothers stared at me.

"You're just fucking with us," Alvaro finally said. "I don't feel anything from that."

Nemesio looked at his brother. "Serious?"

April stood up from the step she had been sitting on and said, "Gas rag them, then."

Even though I had no idea what that meant, I looked at the brothers and said, "Is that what you want? Insulin takes a while to kick in. Do you want the gas?"

"Burn the shits," April said.

Nemesio shook his head. "We'll tell you. We'll tell you. Just promise...you won't hurt us."

"Promise," I said. "Now tell me."

Nemesio looked at his brother, then at me. "We took her to a house in Angeles. On Calle Tabaco."

Alvaro was giving his head tiny, little shakes.

"What's that mean?" I asked him. "You didn't take her there?"

Alvaro said, "No. We didn't."

Nemesio turned to him. "What? Yes, we did."

"We took her to a warehouse in Patria," Alvaro said.

Nemesio leaned toward his brother, straining the handcuffs holding him to the chair. "What the fuck, Alvaro?" Nemesio snapped his head to me. "The house was across from a field. I don't remember the address. It was on Calle Tabaco."

"Don't listen to him," Alvaro argued.

Nemesio turned back to Alvaro. "We have to tell 'em," he yelled. "They're going to fucking burn us like that guy in the Rio."

Alvaro met my gaze. "He doesn't remember the house number because he's fucking with you."

"No, I'm not," Nemesio cried.

"This is a joke," Carlos muttered.

April ducked under the staircase and pulled several dirty rags from the boxes. "Hey," she called out, holding them up, bunched in a fist, "you want the truth?"

I nodded, and she tossed the rags to Ashley. She then reached under the stairs again and pulled a gas can from behind the boxes. "This'll get you the truth."

"This is the *truth*," Nemesio cried. "On Calle Tabaco. Across from a field. There's graffiti on the front door. A big thirty-nine. We took her there and left."

I looked at Nemesio, then Alvaro. Alvaro was still shaking his head.

"He's lying?" I asked. "Your brother is lying?"

"He's lying," Alvaro said, puffing his chest out. "Was a warehouse on the other side of the city."

April came up next to me, holding the gas can.

"You're both lying," I decided and pointed at Nemesio. "Burn him first."

"Listen to me," Nemesio shouted. "I'm telling you! We took her to Angeles!" He turned to Alvaro. "Why are you doing this?"

Carlos uncuffed Nemesio and spun him around, so

he was sitting on the chair backwards. He then grabbed at Nemesio's bound wrists, but the brother pulled away, clutching his hands hard against his stomach.

"No. Don't," Nemesio cried.

Carlos whipped him across the face with the handcuffs, then yanked Nemesio's hands through a gap in the back of the chair. He cuffed him again as Nemesio started to cry.

Ashley tore a thin strip from one of the rags, then another, while April set the gas can on the floor behind Nemesio and pulled out a pocket knife.

"Hold still," she told him before slicing open the back of his shirt, exposing his skin.

"You *really* want this?" I asked Alvaro. "Just tell me where Isa is and this stops."

"I told you where she is."

"Calle Tabaco," Nemesio mumbled.

Alvaro shook his head.

"Fine." I gave April the go-ahead.

She dipped a thin strip of rag into the gas, then lifted it out, dripping, stinking. The fumes spread across the basement as she slapped it on Nemesio's back with a splat.

Ashley handed her a lighter.

"Last chance," April said to the brothers.

"Don't. Please," Nemesio said, wiggling, trying to shake the rag from his back.

Alvaro said nothing.

April shrugged, flicked the lighter, and lit the cloth.

Nemesio screamed.

After a moment, April ripped the burning strip from the brother's back and dropped it to the floor, stamping it out with her boot.

Ashley walked around Nemesio and took a knee to get eye to eye with him. "Where's Isa?" she quietly asked.

"You sick fucks," Nemesio mewled, his back still bubbling.

April slapped down a new strip and lit it, making Nemesio scream even louder. She ripped the strip away and then repeated the process. Again and again.

"You're going to kill him," Alvaro finally cried.

Ashley grabbed the top of Nemesio's head and tilted it up. "Where's Isa?"

"Calle Tabaco," Nemesio said as tears streamed down his face and smoke rose from his back.

"It's the truth," Alvaro cried.

"What is?" I asked.

"We handed her off to a guy in Angeles. Nemesio's telling the truth."

April dipped another rag into the gas can and slapped it on Nemesio's back.

"It's the fucking truth," Alvaro screamed. "We gave her to a trafficker there."

"Who?" Ashley asked.

"Jonathan?" I yelled.

"Luis Galindo," Alvaro said. "Talk to Luis. He'll know where she is."

"Luis lives on Tabaco?" Ashley asked.

"I don't know. I don't think so. He's in Angeles, though. I'll get him to meet you."

"Get him to come here," Carlos said.

Alvaro nodded. "Yeah, sure. I'll call him up." He glanced at his brother, who was struggling to maintain consciousness. "Take him to a hospital, will you? Please."

"No," I said. "Nobody leaves."

"But I'll get Luis. I'll get him here," Alvaro assured me.

"Then get him."

"I will," Alvaro repeated, "but Nemes needs help. Look at his fucking back."

It was a charred, blistering hunk of bacon. But I wasn't sending him anywhere. I leaned into Alvaro's face and said, "Better get Luis here fast."

~

Even upstairs in the kitchen, the smell of burned flesh was strong. I washed my face in the sink, then stared out the window at the shrubs scattered in the rocks and the sand. Everything looked as if it was on the edge of life.

Alvaro was whining about Luis not answering, telling April to try him again. "You have to call him like four or five times. He never answers."

She came up by me where the reception worked and dialed the number Alvaro had given us. "Nope," she said once again before heading back downstairs.

"He'll answer," Alvaro wailed.

The phone in my pocket began to ring, and I reached for the distraction. "Yeah?"

"You didn't show up at the airport," Ingeniero said.

"No. I told you. I'm finding Isa."

"You're making a mistake."

"Luis Galindo," I said.

"What about Galindo?"

"Do you know him?"

"I do," Ingeniero said.

"You didn't tell me about him."

"What would've I told you?"

"Don't mess with me," I said.

Ingeniero was silent for a moment, then said, "Hermanos de la Muerte. Time to let them go."

"What?" My vision blackened around the edges. I wobbled. "How do you know?" I grabbed the counter to steady myself. "Let them go? No. No. No."

"You're playing with fire," Ingeniero explained.

"I'm not letting them go. Not *now*."

"Now."

A rush of adrenaline cleared my head, and I punched the cupboard beside the window. "No," I yelled. "They killed my family. They know where Isa is."

"Isa won't be found," Ingeniero said quietly, confidently. "You're only upsetting the balance of things."

"The balance? Fuck the balance. They gave Isa to Luis. We're calling him now."

"Those idiot kids think that making *you* think they know where she is will be good for them. They have no clue."

"They know! I know they know," I said. "They aren't lying."

"No?"

"No. They're not lying. Not anymore."

"I'm afraid to ask what you did to them."

"They told me where she is."

"Then I'm sending someone to pick them up. Have them ready. I'm sure medical attention is required."

"I'm not—"

Ingeniero hung up.

I threw the phone aside and pulled the Beretta from my waistband. "You're not taking them."

Ashley was at the sink in the back corner and looked over her shoulder as I came storming down into the basement.

"No one's stopping me," I growled.

Carlos popped out from under the stairs, a few unused rags in his hand.

April was next to him, the gas can at her feet. "What'd you say?" she asked.

I marched over to Alvaro and struck him across the face with the butt of the gun. "We're leaving. *Now*. Carry your brother." I turned to Carlos. "Where's the key? Uncuff them."

He cocked his head. "What's going on?"

"They can't stay here," I said. "We have to move them."

"Where?" Carlos pulled the key from his pocket.

"I don't know. I don't care." I stepped around Alvaro and grabbed the handcuffs holding him to the chair. I shouted to Carlos, "Give me the key."

Ashley turned off the faucet with a squeak and wiped her hands on her shirt. "Why do we have to move them?"

I ignored her, yelling at Carlos, "The key."

Carlos took a hesitant step closer to me, squeezing the key between his fingers. "We don't want to move them."

"We have to go!"

April asked, "Why?"

"Quit asking questions! Ingeniero's sending someone."

Carlos's eyes widened. "Shit."

"No shit, shit."

Ashley let out a groan. "We're in serious trouble."

I threw Alvaro's wrists aside and stepped toward Carlos. "Give me the key. Give it."

Upstairs, the back door opened, and the air around us went whistling toward the visitor.

I stretched my hand out. "Give it."

The visitor came to the top of the stairs, only a set of black boots visible. The boots paused for a moment, then started to descend, carefully, deliberately. A figure dressed in black, a face hidden in the shadows, stopped halfway down the staircase.

I pointed the Beretta at the shadow and yelled, "Who the fuck are you?"

The figure took another slow step so he could get in the light, then raised a pair of wrinkled hands. It was just an old man.

"Get out of here," I yelled.

"Wish I could, kid." The man's eyes were nearly hidden under drooping brows. "Ingeniero sent me, though. Name's Trejo." His voice came out in an even hush. With hands still raised, he pointed with a finger. "Those the Davilo brothers?"

"You're not taking them," I yelled. "Get out of here."

Trejo cleared his throat and started to take another step down.

"Don't." I hurried toward the staircase, my gun waving, shaking.

Trejo gave a sigh and said, "I'm not armed, kid."

"Then go away. You can't take them."

The man licked his lips. "Well, I have to, so I'm coming down." He took several slow steps until he'd reached the basement floor. He looked me up and down, his hands in the air, then turned to Carlos. "May I assume that's the key to the cuffs?"

I waved the pistol at Trejo, almost touching his gray cheek with the barrel. "Get out."

Trejo's eyes turned back to me. "Kid, come on."

"You want me to shoot you?"

"You could, but you should know that I didn't come alone."

I swung the gun up the staircase.

"They're outside," Trejo said, "and they're counting. By now, I'd say you've got about ninety seconds until they come in and shoot you all."

"Bullshit," I said, glaring at the man. "Carlos, go look."

"They'll shoot you," Trejo warned. "Anyone other than me and these brothers leave this basement, they'll shoot."

I was hyperventilating, the only sound in the basement coming from the breaths rushing back and forth through my nose.

"Seventy seconds," Trejo said.

"Fuck you," I cried. "Fuck Ingeniero, too." I spun on my heels and put the gun to Nemesio's head.

"Don't," Carlos yelled.

"Sixty seconds," Trejo offered.

"I'll kill them both. Nemesio, then Alvaro," I cried. "I've done it before."

"Fifty seconds."

I turned back to Trejo. "How'd you even get here so fast?" I hissed.

"I wasn't fast. Ingeniero called me an hour ago. I stopped for coffee."

"You can't do this," I cried out, but as I said it, I went storming to the far corner of the basement and pressed my forehead against the wall, shivering. "You can't."

"Give me the key," I heard Trejo say. He then added, "Thank you."

XXIX

The Sicario

Nemesio spent a couple of hours in surgery, the doctors doing what they could, but his burns were so severe that we'd need to take him over to the University Medical Center of El Paso once he stabilized.

I hung around with my parents, just sitting beside Nemesio's bed, getting more and more pissed looking at my dad's face all calm and measured, and then watching my mom, every five minutes, get up and adjust Nemesio's blankets.

I finally said, "He's not even moving. Why do you keep doing that?"

"I just want to be sure," she said, circling the bed for the hundredth time.

"Of what? It was fine the first time, it's fine now."

"I just want to be sure," she said again.

"That's stupid," I grumbled.

As she re-tucked the blanket under Nemesio's arm,

she started to cry.

"Alvaro," my dad said. "Why don't you head home and get some rest?"

"He's not going *home*," my mom said, sniffling. "It's not safe."

"I'm fine," I said. "Nothing will happen. If Miley hadn't opened the door—"

My mom shot me a look. "Don't you blame her."

I shrugged.

"I've got more police patrols tonight," my dad said.

My mom went back to tugging blankets and wiping her eyes.

I looked at him. "Go, then?"

He nodded.

I grabbed his keys from the bedside table and bounced out of there.

Even though I had the strongest urge to go over to Anapra and shoot a few random junkies, I went straight home. I wasn't tired, but I wasn't all that awake either. I fell into the first piece of furniture I came across and just kind of zoned out and watched a street lamp flicker, revealing the sidewalk outside our house in random fits like some old movie reel. A cop car rolled by every hour or so.

When the sky started to turn from black to blue, I got up and made myself a bowl of oats. I couldn't eat it, though. The lumpy, shiny glop looked a little too much like Nemesio's back after the doctor's had worked on him (I'd peaked under the bandages), so I just sat in the kitchen, staring at the fridge until one of my burner phone's began ringing down the hall in my room.

I got to it on the fifth ring. "Yo."

"You didn't check in yesterday," soon-to-be Commissary General Miguel said. "I was worried."

I snorted. "I'm sure you were."

"I was," Miguel said, "and still am. I'm curious what you told them."

"Luis Galindo. That's who we gave Isa to, and that's who we named. No one else; you're safe."

"Did they go after Luis?"

"How would I know?"

"Where's Isa?"

"On her way to Denver."

"Not with Luis?"

"Long gone."

Miguel grunted in satisfaction. "We might still have to do something about Luis, though."

"They don't know the guy."

"They could figure it out. Or Ingeniero could tell them."

"I guess."

"And we should tell your brother about our arrangement...when he recovers."

"It doesn't matter. He's not doing this anymore. He's done."

"He's not done."

"I'm sure of it."

"This isn't a choice. You two work for me."

"He doesn't work for you. I do."

"You're Hermanos de la Muerte. Not Hermano."

"I can't force him to keep doing this."

"You'll have to. Do you know what happens to police informants when they're not police informants anymore?"

"Nothing?"

"Word gets out, and more than just your back gets burned."

"Word won't get out."

"Alvaro, just make sure your brother keeps working with us, okay? Word *always* gets out."

I was quiet as I thought things over.

Miguel said, "Hermanos de la Muerte. Let's keep it that way."

XXX

The Trafficker

I had tipped Ingeniero off to his enforcer's plans with Hermanos de la Muerte. I wanted to show Ingeniero that I had more control of things than he did, and if he was smart, he'd just leave me alone.

Only time would tell if that had worked. I had my doubts.

What had worked, though, was that it had gotten Ingeniero to intervene. The kid had been *so* close to finding his sister, and Ingeniero had cruelly taken that away. Now, I wasn't looking like such the bad guy.

Case in point, the kid was calling me right then.

I answered, feigning ignorance, "You get them?"

"Luis Galindo," the enforcer grumbled. "They said Luis has Isa. Who is that?"

"He's a trafficker down by you."

"I know. He's over in Angeles."

I smiled. "Have the brothers take you to him."

"They're not here."

"You let them go?"

"Ingeniero took them. I need to find Luis."

"So you need my help?"

"I need to find Isa." The desperation in his voice was thick.

I was still smiling. "I can get Luis to meet you somewhere. I'll just tell him he's meeting with me. He'll show."

"Now," the kid said. "Get him to meet me now."

"Yeah, sure, but"—and I drew this out—"since you're on the line, can I ask you for a favor?"

"Anything," he blurted.

My smile grew. This kid would do whatever I asked right about then, so I took the shot and said, "Kill Ingeniero."

There was a pause.

"It's a simple ask," I said. "And I mean, really, he's just a nuisance these days."

"He's an asshole," the enforcer said.

"Exactly. An old guard asshole. So get him out of the way."

"Everything will go to shit."

I laughed. "Worse than it already is?"

"I don't know. Maybe."

"Not a chance. You could even take over. Run things like you want."

"I guess."

"Let me get to work on Luis, and when you tell me Ingeniero has passed into the great beyond, I'll schedule the meeting. You'll have your sister back in no time."

The kid suddenly backtracked. "I can't kill Ingeniero."

"Of course you can."

"But he helped me...once."

"Is he helping you now?"

"No. Maybe he will."

I rolled my eyes. "Let me tell you something about Ingeniero. In case you feel loyal to him, or think he'll come around, let me tell you something, okay? The guy is playing both sides. *Both* sides. He works with the Sinaloa Cartel *and* the Juárez Cartel. Works with AA *and* Aztecas."

"No, he doesn't."

"He sure as hell does. That's why he sent you after me. I found this out."

"He said you traffic kids."

"That's a load of bullshit. He's protecting himself. He's a two-faced son of a bitch."

"He's working with the Aztecas?" the enforcer mumbled.

"How the fuck you think he knows everything he knows? He talks to everyone. And maybe that's why he took the brothers from you. He doesn't want you screwing things up. He'd let your sister die to keep things stable for himself." I let that soak in for a moment, then said, "So listen, I'm going to get you Luis, and you're going to find your sister. Just go kill Ingeniero."

The kid muttered something.

"What?"

"Fine."

"Wonderful. Call me back when you're done."

The line went dead, and I grabbed another burner from a drawer and called Luis. "Got an opportunity for you."

"Yeah? What's that?"

"Ingeniero's enforcer is at 3705 Calle Santiago."

"The address good?"

"Alvaro gave it to me. It's good."

"What's he look like?"

"Big. A little over six foot. Two hundred some pounds. He's a beast."

"I'll head over."

XXXI
The Boy

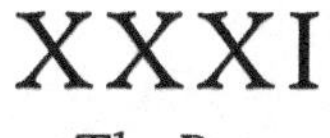

Standing in the house on Santiago with Carlos, I looked out the window, scanning the street. There wasn't much movement. The cars all had a layer of dust on them from having sat through the night. Way down the block, a little girl and her mother were walking, trailed by a stray dog, and an old man watched the procession from his doorway, sipping a coffee.

I turned to Carlos. "Where're the M4s? Dante was picking them up last night, wasn't he?"

Carlos shook his head. "Man, I don't even want to tell you what happened."

"He forget?"

"Ingeniero took them."

I smirked. "No, he didn't. Don't even joke."

"I'm serious." Carlos took a step away from me. "Victor just told me."

"No," I groaned.

"Dante was there, the M4s were there, and then Ingeniero just came riding up with some guys and took everything. Took Dante too. Fucking maniac."

My head drooped. "He *is* working with the Aztecas."

"What's that?"

"I have to kill Ingeniero." I looked up at him and repeated it.

Carlos chuckled, but I wasn't kidding, and when he realized this, his smile dropped. "Are you insane? You can't do that."

"He's fucking everything up."

"You can't just kill Ingeniero."

"I have to."

"You want everything to go to shit?"

"It already is. And what do I care if it means I find Isa?"

"Why would it mean that?"

"Jonathan gets me Luis if I kill him. That's the deal."

"Deal?"

"Jonathan helped me with the Davilos. He'll help me with Isa."

"Are you out of your mind?"

I stepped away from the window.

"You're out of your mind." Carlos followed me across the room. "You can't kill Ingeniero."

"Sure I can." I opened the front door.

"No, you *can't*. As in: don't. Look what happened after you killed Javier. What do you think'll happen if you kill Ingeniero? The Aztecas would tear us apart. The barrio would burn. We'd *all* die."

I shrugged. "But maybe not Isa."

Carlos grabbed my shoulder. "Wait."

I shook him loose.

He grabbed me again, sinking his fingers deep.

"He'll see you coming a mile away."

"Get off me."

Carlos grabbed me with his other hand and tugged. "Dude."

"Let go."

"We'll find another way."

He pulled harder, and I spun around and punched him in the face, knocking him to the ground.

"This is the *only* way," I yelled. "The *only* way."

He looked up, blinking, a hand under his nose where blood was collecting, pooling, ready to spill over his fingers. "You can't do this," he said.

I reached down and pulled the gun from his waist. "Don't follow me."

~

I stopped outside Ingeniero's house and cut the bike's 250cc engine. There was a freshly washed GMC Suburban at the curb.

Maybe Ingeniero had guests.

Maybe there were a bunch of Aztecas inside with him.

Maybe my Beretta and Carlos's gun were both tucked against my back, and I'd kick in the front door and blast away.

Maybe.

Except I hadn't even gotten off the bike when Ingeniero came out. Alone.

He spotted me at the curb. "You change your mind about Salas?"

"I, uh, I want to talk."

He waved at the SUV. "Fine. Let's go for a ride. Talk some."

I looked at him, then the heavily tinted windows of the GMC. "Is that yours?" I asked, but I really wanted to know if there was anyone sitting inside who'd jump out the moment I pulled the guns.

"Just bought it," Ingeniero said.

I carefully got off the bike, the pistols shifting under my waistband.

"Wonderful." Ingeniero locked the door to his house and came down the steps.

I hadn't thought it'd be this easy. I stretched a little, scratched my back, got my hand close to the Beretta.

Ingeniero came right up to me, still smiling. He flicked out his tongue, wetting his lips, looking like a snake. "I was heading over to see your friend, The Gunman."

"He's not my friend."

"I know."

"You shouldn't have cancelled my order."

"We can talk about that. All three of us."

"I can have my guns?"

"I didn't say that."

"But maybe? We can talk?"

"Of course." He gestured to the SUV. "After you."

I brought my hand around. Empty. I could wait.

"I bought this today," Ingeniero said after we'd climbed into the Suburban. "Has this GPS thing"—he pointed at the center console—"but I'm not sure how it works. Some Japanese thing."

I looked over my shoulder to scan the back, just in case.

"It's yours," Ingeniero said, patting me on the leg.

I turned to him. "What's mine?"

"This. The Suburban. You can have it."

"Huh?"

"If you go see Salas."

"After I find Isa."

"You shouldn't be riding around on that bike. Not with the way things are getting. You need something like this if you're going to go roaming around the city looking for your sister. Go see Salas, get this, find your sister."

I was shaking my head. I didn't want to go see Salas. I didn't need the SUV. I wanted my guns. I wanted to find Isa. As Ingeniero started the engine, I asked, "What've you heard about Isa?"

"Nothing, unfortunately. But don't worry."

"Don't worry?"

"I've put out the word: if she's not found alive, people will pay. Be patient. She'll turn up." Ingeniero waited for a car to pass, then pulled from the curb. "Maybe she'll even be found before you get back from Sinaloa." He gave me a sideways look.

He knew I wasn't going to Sinaloa.

He was waiting for me to make my move. He knew why I was there. And the moment I pulled out one of my guns, he was going to strike.

But I could wait too.

So we just sat, and after a few blocks, Ingeniero said, "I'm proud of you. I really thought you were going to kill the Davilo brothers after I'd called. Before Trejo could get there. But you stayed calm. That was good. Calm."

He was driving us down the streets like this was just another errand.

And it was so tempting. If I just pulled a gun...

But I couldn't.

"You'll do good things," Ingeniero continued. "I really think so. Salas does too."

We pulled up to a line of cars waiting to enter the roundabout before the Periférica Camino Real Highway.

Ingeniero drummed his fingers across the top of the steering wheel. "I used to own some racehorses," he said. "I could always tell which ones were going to become winners. Fantastic Piloto was my favorite. I really liked that horse." He gave me another sideways glance. "You're a Fantastic Piloto."

I tried to look at him and grin, to give off a

casualness that matched his, maybe throw him off a little, but I caught sight of a motorcycle rolling up behind us, and I could only scowl.

He laughed. "That's a good thing."

The motorcycle hopped up on the median and came alongside us, stopping just behind Ingeniero's door.

My jaw went slack. "Shit."

"What?" Ingeniero followed my gaze to see the helmeted rider raising a rifle. "Oh, no." Ingeniero slammed his foot on the gas and punched out of the line of traffic, clipping the motorcycle and knocking the sicario to the ground.

I pulled my Beretta and turned around, grabbing my seat for stability, as we raced into the roundabout.

The sicario was already on his feet. He fired twice, catching the back side of the SUV, then pulled his bike upright.

"He's coming," I shouted.

We sped through the roundabout, the tires barely holding on, and took the exit toward Anapra, the slums in the hills outside of Juárez.

Ingeniero had barely straightened the SUV before the sicario came rocketing out of the traffic circle.

I took a shot at the rider, but the SUV was bouncing over so many potholes that I only hit the back seat. I fired again and put a hole in the roof. "Fucking A." I dug my knees into the seat, steadied myself, and shot again. This time, the bullet went through the back window, but I couldn't tell where it'd gone after that.

The sicario was holding back, though.

I looked over my shoulder at the road ahead. We were cresting the hill that looked down upon the Anapra barrio. On both sides of us, small, vandalized huts were scattered among the sand and shrubs.

"Where do we go?"

"There's—"

Bullets hit the back of the SUV, sinking into the sheet metal with quick thumps.

"Hold him off," Ingeniero yelled.

I turned and took another shot, but that was all I could do before the sicario returned a volley of bullets, and I had to duck.

One of the rear tires exploded.

"Christ," Ingeniero shouted, wrestling with the wheel.

I reached over to help hold it steady, but the SUV touched the edge of the road, and the steering wheel ripped from both our hands.

We went into a spin. We clipped something. A shack. A sheet of corrugated metal. Something heavy smashed into the windshield, and Ingeniero's airbag deployed, pinning him hard against his seat.

Nothing deployed on my side, and I got tossed around like a doll. My face slammed against the window. My head hit the seatback, then the door frame. I might've blacked out.

The next thing I knew, we were stopped, half buried in a sand dune that had piled up against the side of another shack. Dust swirled around us. My Beretta was missing.

I held my hand against my face, feeling the blood dribbling through my fingers. There was a tap on my window. I turned my eyes.

The sicario had his rifle aimed at my head. He made a quick gesture with the gun.

I looked at Ingeniero, trapped—the sand dune outside his door and the airbag still half inflated.

"What do I do?" I asked.

He blinked, squinted at me, then the helmeted rider. "Roll your window down. Let me talk to him."

I nodded. I showed the sicario my empty hands, then tried the window. "It doesn't work."

Ingeniero said, "Then open the door."

I kept my eyes locked on the sicario's visor and carefully pushed the door open a crack.

"All the way," Ingeniero instructed.

I did, and the sicario stepped back, the rifle still pointed at me.

"What's your name?" Ingeniero asked.

"Get out," the sicario said.

Ingeniero faked a chuckle. "I'm a bit stuck."

"Not you. Him," the sicario said.

I turned to Ingeniero.

"Do as he asks."

I slowly dropped from the SUV. A wind had picked up that was clearing the air of the dust we'd disturbed. In the sicario's black visor, I could see myself, the SUV, and Ingeniero.

"Jonathan sent me," the sicario said.

I glanced over my shoulder at Ingeniero, a smile across my face.

"What'd he say? I couldn't hear him. What's your name?"

I stepped aside and gave the sicario a clear shot.

XXXII

The Boy

After the sicario rode off, I reached into the SUV, keeping my head down so I wouldn't have to see what the AK-47 had done to Ingeniero, and found the Beretta I'd lost in a pile of broken glass. I tucked it into my waistband next to Carlos's gun.

Eyes from the darkened huts around me watched as I headed for the road and called Jonathan.

"He's dead," I said.

"Yeah. Just got the message."

I switched the phone to my other ear, so it wouldn't press into my split cheek. "Where's Luis?"

"You know, technically, *you* didn't kill Ingeniero," Jonathan said.

"Where's Luis?" I repeated.

"At 7926 Petunia," Jonathan said. "It's off Bernardo Norzagaray Boulevard."

I shoved the phone into my pocket and went

sprinting onto the highway, jumping in front of the first car that came over the hill, some beat-up Pontiac Sunfire. After yanking out the middle-aged driver, I turned the car around and raced back down the highway, hitting the roundabout so fast that the creaky Pontiac started to drift. At the Bernardo Norzagaray exit, I veered off, gunning it again, pushing the car up and into the winding dirt roads of Angeles.

The house, 7926 Petunia, was some neglected place on an overlook with a sweeping view of the University of Texas–El Paso across the border.

I skidded into the cinder block wall out front and burst from the car, scrambling over the crumbled mess and throwing myself at the house's sun-bleached door. The frame cracked, but the thing held, so I drew back, raised a foot, and gave it the hardest kick I could, snapping the bolt and hinges clear off.

I fired two shots into the ceiling, one from the Beretta and one from Carlos's gun, and swung the weapons around the room.

But it was empty. There was nothing there. No furniture, no Luis, nothing at 7926 Petunia but dust.

And something small on the greasy carpet that faintly shined in the sunlight sneaking through the doorway.

The plastic was clean and new. The little jewels dotting the front of it winked at me. It was a red tiara, almost identical to the tiara I had given Isa, mocking and taunting.

Isa wasn't there, but I still went rushing through the small house, searching for her.

"What the fuck is this shit?" I screamed at Jonathan when he answered my call.

"You bent the other one pretty bad, so I got you a new one."

I was back in the front room and kicked the tiara, tiny jewels flying everywhere. "Where's Luis?"

"Sorry, kid. You could've killed Ingeniero. You didn't. No deal."

"What's it matter? Ingeniero's dead. Where is Luis?"

"I'm not giving up Luis. He's an even better sicario than he is a trafficker."

"He killed Ingeniero?"

"Damn skippy. So good luck with finding your sister."

I was grinding my teeth so hard that the split in my cheek started bleeding again. "I'll kill you."

"Hey, you do that," Jonathan laughed, "but Luis doesn't have your sister anyway. He left her at a drop. She's long gone."

"I'm going to kill you."

"Or," Jonathan said, "you could get those Davilo brothers back. They know a lot more than they're letting on. I guarantee you that."

"They're gone."

"They're *not* gone. Ingeniero is, though, and now nobody's going to be protecting those idiots. You could do whatever you want to them."

I snarled into the phone, "Fuck you," but the man was right, and I sprinted out to the Pontiac.

~

The homes behind the Davilos were set on top of each other, only enough space between them for cement walls. I paced up and down the sidewalk, trying to find a gap where I could sneak through.

Some kids were playing in one of the backyards, kicking a soccer ball, and every thump of the ball made my head throb. I clutched my temples and paced, going from house to dividing wall to house, and back. The brothers' house was right there—I could see its blue-gray roof tiles—

but I couldn't find a way to get through.

I finally just gave up and pulled myself atop one of the walls. The space was only big enough for a little kid (like Isa), but I forced myself in, the homes pressing against me on both sides, their rooflines reaching over my head. I was crouching, bent over into a ball, but I went barreling into the gap anyway.

Momentum kept me from getting stuck as burning hot roof tiles scraped my head and stucco scratched at my shoulders and hips. Fabric tore. Tiles fell behind me, crashing onto the wall. The space somehow got tighter, but just as I started to think I wouldn't make it through, the houses fell away and open sky appeared above me.

I stood, teetering between green lawns, the brothers' house in front of me.

One of the kids said, "Check that guy out," while the other kicked the soccer ball around him and scored.

Alvaro and his parents were sitting around a glass table, talking quietly, tucked away in their walled patio. Alvaro said something to his father, then snickered like things were perfect.

I went racing along the top of the wall. Alvaro glanced up and saw me, but I was already leaping over their wall's razor wire and the deflated ball stuck in it.

I hit the grass with a thud, rolled, and bounced up. Alvaro's mother cried out, spilling her water, as I pulled my gun.

Alvaro, a vicious bruise across the side of his face and dark rings around his eyes, froze the second I pointed the Beretta at his head, hissing, "Fucking stay there." I came up to the patio's edge and waved the gun at all of them. "Stay there."

Alvaro's father put his hands flat on the table. His mother sat sniveling, ignoring the water dripping off the table into her lap.

"Now get up," I told Alvaro. "Slow."

The brother looked at his father.

The man nodded. "Go ahead."

Alvaro's eyes widened. "You serious?"

The man nodded again. "It'll be fine."

"Get up," I demanded.

Alvaro shook his head, but he still stood, nudging his chair back, grating the metal against the patio's stone.

I circled the table and grabbed him by the neck, jamming the pistol into his temple.

A sad mewling sound escaped his mother's lips, and his father said, "Be calm. Just everyone be calm."

I jerked Alvaro toward the house and shoved him against the back door. "Open it." As he fumbled with the knob, my hand still on his neck, I turned to his parents and waved the gun at them. "Stay there."

His mother began to sob. Alvaro got the door open, and I marched him inside, kicking the door shut behind us, cutting the woman off.

"Where's the garage?" I asked, scanning the all-white kitchen around us.

Alvaro pointed to a door across the room.

"Keys? Car keys."

"There," Alvaro said. "On the counter."

I pushed him toward the garage, grabbing the keys as we passed.

"What do you even want?" Alvaro asked.

"You know."

There were two vehicles in the garage, the Mercedes I'd seen before and a red Jeep Wrangler. The keys had a Jeep logo on them, so I forced Alvaro over to the Wrangler. "You're driving," I said, pushing him from the passenger seat to the driver's side.

I turned and shot the front tire of the Mercedes, then climbed into the Jeep. "Drive," I said, tossing the keys into his lap.

"This isn't going to work," he said, pressing the

garage opener. "You're going to die. I know people."

"Cristo de Curiel."

"What?"

"Drive to Cristo de Curiel."

"That's, like, twenty minutes away."

"I don't care."

"Whatever. Your funeral." He backed out of the garage, and neither of us said another word until we'd reached the Rio Grande and Alvaro had turned west.

"Heard your sister died," he said.

"She's not dead."

"You're chasing a ghost."

"You better hope not."

"You want to know how she died?"

I ignored him.

"You want to know if it was quick?"

I didn't answer.

"It wasn't."

I shook my head. He was lying. I knew he was lying. He had to be lying.

"Diabetes messed her up."

"Shut the fuck up," I croaked.

Alvaro was quiet for a minute, then asked, "How far you think we'll get before the police spot us?" He adjusted the rearview mirror. "My parents called 'em. They're out looking for us right now."

I pressed the barrel of the gun hard into Alvaro's bruised cheek, causing him to wince. "Drive faster, then."

The Jeep accelerated, and despite Alvaro's warning, we safely reached the roundabout near Angeles and turned onto the Periférica Camino Real Highway. The city fell back and the desert opened up around us. The sun disappeared behind the mountains to the west. I turned around and watched the roundabout, eyeing the vehicles circling it. One exited and came up the highway, and it kind of looked like a large military truck, but with its headlights on, I couldn't tell.

I glanced at the road ahead of us. "Turn," I said. "Turn here."

"This isn't Cristo."

"Turn," I shouted.

Alvaro hit the brakes and yanked the wheel, taking us onto a rough utility road.

I looked back, waiting for the truck's headlights to appear, but I didn't see anything through the cloud of dust the Jeep was kicking up.

I let Alvaro drive for another five minutes before I told him to pull over. "Off the road. Over there." I pointed at a flat spot.

"You're not getting away with this," he said, taking the Jeep into the open area.

I pointed at the abandoned mine to our left.

"What? Is that your lair, you troll?"

"You're staying here until you tell me where Isa is."

"I told you," Alvaro groaned. "She's dead. Isa *is* dead. We took her. She was wearing white pajama bottoms and a Mickey Mouse shirt. We gave her to Luis, but then she died. Fucking Christ, man."

My hand tightened around the gun as some weird, raspy growling came up from deep within my throat.

Alvaro drew back.

I said, "Where is—"

But a burst of automatic gunfire cracked through the desert air.

The truck that'd come out of the roundabout was sitting on the dirt road with a soldier standing in the bed, a rifle over the roof aimed at us.

"Ha! Told you," Alvaro said. "My dad called the fucking army."

I punched him in the jaw, then reached over his lap and opened the door. As he howled, clutching his face, I shoved him out, then scrambled over the seat and dragged us both to the dirt.

The soldier called out to us.

I peeked around the Jeep's bumper. Two more men had appeared, their rifles on the hood of the truck. The soldier in the back flipped on a spotlight.

I pulled back, blinded, blinking until the spot had faded.

"You're dead," Alvaro chortled.

I scanned the desert around us for a way out, but everything—the shrubs, the mine, the broken elevator (just a hole in the ground), the embankment around us—was glowing from the spotlight, and there was nowhere to go.

So I went for the light. I swung around and fired, but I only managed to put two bullets in the side of the truck before the soldiers fired back, and I had to dive for cover, their bullets sinking into the Jeep, puncturing steel and shattering glass.

Alvaro laughed when one of the tires blew out with a sharp hiss.

I punched him in the gut, then scrambled to the back of the Jeep.

The soldiers stopped.

I counted to five, then went for the spotlight again. On this side, the light wasn't shining right at me, and I only needed one shot. The spotlight sparked excitedly, then died.

The soldiers adjusted their aim and opened fire again.

"You're dead," Alvaro cried over the barrage.

"Where's Isa?" I shouted.

"Dead," Alvaro yelled. "Both of you. Dead."

Smoke was swirling around us. The truck had caught fire.

Alvaro got in my face. "Dead!"

I grabbed him by the collar and shoved him to the dirt.

He was grinning, shouting, "Dead! Dead! Dead!"

I shoved my pistol into his mouth, and just as I was going to pull the trigger, a helicopter crested the ridge behind the mine, passing overhead, then settling above the soldiers, a great cloud of sand rising into the air around it. A spotlight snapped to life, and the world became filled with an eerie haze.

Alvaro scrambled to his feet and tried to run to the soldiers, but I grabbed him and jerked him back, tossing him to the sand.

"Stay there."

He bounced back up, planting his legs in a ready stance. "Fuck you, you troll," he spat, then took off in the opposite direction.

I went sprinting after him, nearly losing him in the dust and smoke before his hazy figure vanished into the mine. My mine.

~

Alvaro probably thought he could lose me in there, but he had no clue how many times I'd visited the place. When the darkness overtook us, he began bumping and clawing along while I came up fast and kicked the back of his leg, sending him crumpling in a heap.

"Get off me," he screamed.

"Shut the fuck up."

"Get off! Ah!"

I knocked him on the head several times until there was only the wind pouring into the mine from the helicopter's blades.

I lifted the brother to his feet and shoved him farther into the darkness.

"In here," he yelled, his voice echoing around us. "I'm in—"

I cracked him across the back of the head so hard he dropped to a knee.

"In—"

I hit him again, and he fell to his side, moaning.

Then the world around us flashed white.

"Over here," Alvaro cried.

The beams of light focused on us, and a voice yelled, "Lay down your weapon."

I turned around, shielding my eyes, but the lights were so bright, so blinding that I could only see a glowing fog.

"Lay down your weapon."

The voice was closer. A shape was hovering just outside my reach. A rifle had to be pointed at my head.

"Now!"

I dropped the Beretta, and it clattered to the stone and dirt. The nearest light snapped away, shining the pitted wall, and the soldier stepped forward.

He kicked the pistol aside as another came around and grabbed my wrists, pulled them behind my back, and bound them with a zip tie. The soldier then did the same to Alvaro.

"Are you joking?" Alvaro whined. "Are you an idiot?"

The soldier said nothing.

"My dad's Enrique Davilo."

"We'll verify that," the soldier said.

"Screw you," Alvaro said.

The soldiers marched us out of the mine.

XXXIII

The Sicario

"**S**he *is* dead, you piece of shit."

The Beast and I were sitting in the back of the military truck, the sound of the helicopter fading.

"We took her to Luis, and she *died*."

I leaned over, trying to see the idiot's face, trying to see some signal that he was listening, but there didn't seem to be any life in him anymore.

I sat back, grinning, wondering if maybe I should tell him that I was lying, that his sister was actually alive. Nothing the idiot could do about it now. And it'd kill him. I'd tell him that Nemesio and I had dumped the girl on Luis, he'd passed her off to Mike, and Mike was now halfway to Albuquerque, having just left that middle-of-nowhere place called Truth or Consequences. "Yep," I could say. "She's somewhere out there, alive. Honest."

I gave a sideways glance at the lump beside me. His skin had grown pale and sweaty. His arms hung slack from his wide shoulders. He blinked once, slow.

"You fucking troll."

I *so* wanted to tell him, but I held my tongue. I wasn't risking the deal I had with Miguel. The girl had to make it to Denver, so he could get his big bust with all his FBI buddies, and I could get a crazy payout. Miguel, apparently, had access to funds, significant funds, for informants.

Because of this, I *was* actually a little worried about the girl, ironically. It sounded like she was in pretty bad shape. Mike said it was like he was dragging a body to Albuquerque. The girl was a zombie, just in a daze. I had told him it probably had something to do with her diabetes, so he'd loaded her up on soda and shit, but she'd just gotten worse, so who the hell knew?

I remembered The Beast saying his sister needed insulin, so maybe that was part of the diabetes deal, but then again, he'd also tried to kill me with insulin, so whatever. I just hoped she'd survive the next thirty-six hours and get to Denver so Miguel could do his thing and Nemesio and I could keep doing ours.

Hermanos de la Muerte.

XXXIV

The Boy

A soldier pulled me and Alvaro from the truck, lined us up next to each other, then stood behind us, a hand on each of our shoulders as a white Mercedes pulled up.

The tire I had shot had been replaced with a spare.

"Finally," Alvaro grumbled.

His father, Enrique, got out and looked over the roof at us. He nodded to his son.

Some round-faced police officer dressed in a crisp uniform—collared shirt and tucked tie—climbed out the passenger side. The seven-pointed star over the man's chest meant he was with the Federal Police, so when he looked at the soldier and said, "Let him go," the soldier cut the zip tie binding Alvaro's wrists.

The brother gave a satisfied sigh and smiled at me as he went walking over to the Mercedes.

Enrique came around the car to meet him. "You okay?"

"Fine," Alvaro muttered.

"You don't look fine." Enrique brushed some dust from his son's hair.

Alvaro leaned away. "I'm fine."

"Okay." Enrique stuck his hands in his pocket and looked around.

The cloud kicked up by the helicopter hadn't quite drifted away, and with the darkening sky, the desert outside the mine had grown dim and faded. The mine behind the Mercedes was just a dark spot in the haze, and the elevator shaft (just an unguarded hole that I wanted them all to just slip into and vanish) couldn't even be seen.

Enrique turned to me. "You look worse than the bodies you guys hang from the bridges."

I felt like it.

My head throbbed. My skin was cold, but I was sweating. And I was nauseous. And weak, and breathless, and aching. Aching everywhere. I felt like death.

My eyes drifted to the sky.

Enrique said, "Maybe we should just leave him out here to crawl into a hole and die."

"Your call," the officer said. "I don't care either way."

I started to wobble, to sway, becoming more lightheaded and groggy, almost like how Isa used to say her lows felt. And I welcomed it. Whatever took me away from this hell and let me fade into nothing, I welcomed it.

"If I knew he'd suffer, I would," Enrique said.

I brought my eyes down to the group by the Mercedes.

The officer was looking off into the distance. "You do what you want. I'm not stopping you."

"Hey," Alvaro said, trying to get my attention. "Hey."

I looked at him, but not really. I couldn't clear myself of the fog.

Alvaro came over, wiggling his finger like he had a secret to tell me. He grabbed my elbow, pulled me down to his level, and whispered, "Nemesio and I, we'd kill them all again. We really would." He tapped a finger against my temple. "Pop... pop... pop." He stared me straight in the face and smiled wide. "Just know that."

I tried to pull myself back from wherever I was floating off to.

"Oh, and you know what?" Alvaro patted my pockets, found Isa's insulin, and took it out. "How about I pump *you* full of this shit, huh?" He clutched the vial in his fist and turned around to his father, saying, "This is what the fucker stuck me with."

My eyes regained their focus, and I stopped swaying. For the first time in days, I stood calm as something rushed through me, telling me to fight, telling me to break through the zip tie and fight.

My shoulders tensed, and I strained my arms, my wrists, clenching my teeth, spit flying from my lips, the zip tie digging into my skin, cutting, gouging, and then snapping away.

The soldier clamped down on my shoulder, but I threw him off, and as Enrique reached out for his son, I lowered my head and drove hard into Alvaro's back, causing a panicked puff of air to shoot from his lungs.

I lifted the small sicario from the ground, dug my feet into the sand, and carried Alvaro across the desert until the earth below us just disappeared.

Gone.

Vanished.

Alvaro and I tumbled over the edge of the elevator shaft, weightless for a second, then stopped hard against the top of the rusted cage with a *boom*. Alvaro's leg smacked against something, maybe the boulder I'd heaved down days ago, and he screamed.

I rolled onto my back, gasping, the wind knocked

out of me, gazing up at the dark, crimson sky beyond the opening. I could see a star, or maybe a planet way, way up there.

The cage groaned.

I reached for Alvaro's hand, searching for Isa's insulin, but he had to have dropped it. There was nothing there.

Someone shined a flashlight into the shaft.

"Shoot him," Enrique yelled. "Shoot him, and get my son out of there!"

I stared up at the light, focusing on it, letting my mind race, thinking of my family, of Isa, of Katie, of Mom, of Grandma, of Dad. I thought of how I'd tried. Tried to help. Tried to make money. Tried to make things safe. I thought of my house on the hill. The city it overlooked.

The cage stayed in place for a moment longer, a million thoughts coming and going, but then the metal buckled, broke free from the wall, and plunged us into darkness.

EPILOGUE

The ABQ Game Ranger

"Ten-four. In route." I clicked the radio back in place and turned the truck down the perimeter road behind the Albuquerque airport. Breathing deep, a bit of bile rising in the back of my throat, I tried not to think about what was down there. The worst things always seemed to happen whenever I was out in the field, though.

I pulled up behind a Kirtland Air Force Base utility truck, and I was shaking. I couldn't help it.

"Nine-oh-five on scene," I radioed before getting out.

A tan, leathery man in a loose yellow vest got out of the truck and drifted toward me. He pointed at a clump of shadscale in the desert twenty yards off. The sock, bright red, was easy to spot. "Didn't think I should disturb her," the man said. "Crime scene, right?"

Being exposed to the elements like the body was, it probably didn't matter, but I said, "That's good, sir. Thank you."

I tucked my sunglasses into my shirt pocket and made my way toward the bush that was just starting to bloom.

Underneath the wild, creeping branches was a little body, a child, her skinny legs sticking out, a red sock on one foot, the other bare.

I could smell the blossoms, which was strange. Bodies smelled. And they got bad fast in the sun, but this one, maybe because it was so small, wasn't giving off much of anything.

I reached out and pushed aside the branches to get a look at the girl's face. She was seven or eight years old. Black hair. Eyes closed, ringed with wide, dark circles. The skin across her face was badly sunburned, blistered and stretched over tiny cheekbones. The birthmark on her cheek was still clear, though. That would help with identification.

I knelt down, one hand still holding back the branches, and pressed my other hand against the girl's neck. Just in case.

And there was a pulse.

THANK YOU

I hope you enjoyed *Isa's Insulin*.

If you'd like to leave a review, that would mean the world to me.

~ Chester

ABOUT THE AUTHOR

I write stories for public consumption. If you'd like to follow me on social media, I'm on Instagram and Twitter.

I also have a website where you can sign up for my mailing list, which will get you book release notifications, sample chapters, discounts, and more.

www.Instagram.com/ChesterGattle

www.Twitter.com/ChesterGattle

www.ChesterGattle.com